"The Journey To Your Heart, And Your Bed, Is A Difficult One."

"Do you always have to come straight to the point?" Rose asked. Leaning against the front-porch post, his cotton shirt unbuttoned above his crossed arms and wearing jeans like any other Waterville male, Stefan took her breath away.

Rose forced herself back to the garden of reason, picking out the weeds of temptation. She'd known him for only two weeks; he came from a different world. He would be leaving, once boredom hit him—or summer ended.

"Yes, I do always come to the point."

She stared meaningfully at Stefan. He looked more like lover material than a husband. Rose didn't want to dip into dreams safely tucked away. "I think you'd better leave."

"Very well. But I want you to think about this—I have waited too long for a woman like you. The single women of Waterville have started hunting me, and I want you to call them off. I cannot oblige the not-so-subtle invitations to their beds, because I intend to be in yours."

Dear Reader,

Welcome to the world of Silhouette Desire, where you can indulge yourself every month with romances that can only be described as passionate, powerful and provocative!

Silhouette's beloved author Annette Broadrick returns to Desire with a MAN OF THE MONTH who is *Hard To Forget*. Love rings true when former high school sweethearts reunite while both are on separate undercover missions to their hometown. Bestselling writer Cait London offers you *A Loving Man,* when a big-city businessman meets a country girl and learns the true meaning of love.

The Desire theme promotion THE BABY BANK, about sperm-bank client heroines who find love unexpectedly, returns with Amy J. Fetzer's *Having His Child*, part of her WIFE, INC. miniseries. The tantalizing Desire miniseries THE FORTUNES OF TEXAS: THE LOST HEIRS continues with *Baby of Fortune* by Shirley Rogers. In *Undercover Sultan,* the second book of Alexandra Sellers's SONS OF THE DESERT: THE SULTANS trilogy, a handsome prince is forced to go on the run with a sexy mystery woman—who may be the enemy. And Ashley Summers writes of a Texas tycoon who comes home to find a beautiful stranger living in his mansion in *Beauty in His Bedroom*.

This month see inside for details about our exciting new contest "Silhouette Makes You a Star." You'll feel like a star when you delve into all six fantasies created in Desire books this August!

Enjoy!

Joan Marlow Golan

Joan Marlow Golan
Senior Editor, Silhouette Desire

Please address questions and book requests to:
Silhouette Reader Service
U.S.: 3010 Walden Ave., P.O. Box 1325, Buffalo, NY 14269
Canadian: P.O. Box 609, Fort Erie, Ont. L2A 5X3

Cait London

A LOVING MAN

Published by Silhouette Books

America's Publisher of Contemporary Romance

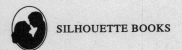 **SILHOUETTE BOOKS**

ISBN 0-373-76382-4

A LOVING MAN

Books by Cait London

CAIT LONDON

lives in the Missouri Ozarks but loves to travel the Northwest's gold rush/cattle drive trails every summer. She enjoys research trips, meeting people and going to Native American dances. Ms. London is an avid reader who loves to paint, play with computers and grow herbs (particularly scented geraniums right now). She's a national bestselling and award-winning author, and she has also written historical romances under another pseudonym. Three is her lucky number; she has three daughters, and the events in her life have always been in threes. "I love writing for Silhouette," Cait says. "One of the best perks about all this hard work is the thrilling reader response and the warm, snug sense that I have given readers an enjoyable, entertaining gift."

SILHOUETTE MAKES YOU A STAR!
Feel like a star with Silhouette.
Look for the exciting details of our new contest
inside all of these fabulous Silhouette novels:

One

"**Y**ou're old-fashioned and don't know what it is to be young." His daughter's words raked Stefan Donatien; their argument of the early morning still scalded him. "You can't keep me as a child forever," Estelle had said furiously.

Brooding about her temper, a match to his own, Stefan had escaped the farmhouse he had just purchased. His mission into Waterville, a small Midwestern town, provided a time in which to recover and reshape his defenses. His mother, Yvette, often agreed with Estelle. A man alone against a volatile, twenty-year-old daughter, and his French mother, Stefan often had to find "caves" into which to retreat. They loved him, and he returned that love, but his women could be difficult at times, united against him.

Though he was born in the United States, his daughter and French-born mother, Yvette, often accused him of being "old-world." "Perhaps if you had a lover, you would not be so obsessed with keeping Estelle a child," his mother had stated. "You may have buried your heart with your wife, Claire, but you did not bury your life. At your age, I was already a *grandmère* and I did not stop living when your father passed on. You are only forty-two, and yet you are old before your time. See there? A gray hair."

Stefan inhaled the early May air and tried to settle his raw nerves, raked by the formidable women he loved deeply. They might see him as an overbearing tyrant, but every instinct he possessed told him to protect them.

He listened to the rumbling of the old pickup's engine as he cruised into Waterville. The ancient farm pickup suited the rural Missouri town much better than the luxury car he'd used in Chicago. The small community, wedged amid the surrounding farms and rolling green mountains, was the perfect place in which to protect his daughter from Louie, alias The Freeloader.

Stefan scowled at the truck's rearview mirror and at his right temple; his single gray hair gleamed, mocking him. In many ways, he felt as battered as the pickup that came with the Smith's farm. It was only a matter of time before Louie took Estelle as a lover. To avoid that, Stefan had decided to give his daughter the one thing she'd always wanted—the experience of living in a small, Midwestern American town.

Stefan's old pickup prowled by Waterville's vegetable gardens lined with new green plants. Heavy with morning dew, pink and white peonies leaned against the picket fences and shade trees bordered the streets. A yellow school bus stopped to pick up children clustered on the sidewalk. Seated on their porch swings, women with curlers in their gray hair whispered about the new owner of the Smith farm as he passed. A widower with a slight accent, a beautiful twenty-year-old daughter and an enchanting, happy French mother was certain to be noticed.

It was only the third day since Stefan had moved his family to the rural community. With the exception of clashing with him over Estelle's adult status, they seemed happy. It wasn't easy uprooting his family and moving them to the safety of the small town. But then Stefan was a powerful businessman who knew how to make decisions, especially when his daughter was endangered. As soon as Estelle's college finals were over, Stefan had put his plan to protect his daughter into motion. A trusted friend and employee now managed the restaurant line that Stefan's father had begun, Donatien's French Cuisine Restaurants.

His father, Guy, would have dealt harshly with Estelle, just as he had with his boy, Stefan, demanding perfection and obedience.

Stefan smiled tightly, remembering his father and better understanding the fear that sometimes ruled a parent. Guy had wanted the best for Stefan, just as Stefan wanted the best for Estelle.

He inhaled abruptly. *Though he loved his father, he did not favor Guy's strict parental control and too high standards. Stefan had promised himself not to be so exacting and controlling with his daughter. He wasn't happy that his protective-father-mode sometimes erupted into just that—"I forbid you" sounded exactly like his father.* His headache started to throb in rhythm to the rumble of the old vehicle's engine.

A horde of young boys on bicycles soared past him, and Stefan braked slowly. Beneath the ball caps turned backward on their heads, their expressions were wary and curious of the new stranger. Even the dog, running at their side, noted Stefan's presence with excited barking.

*At least Estelle was safe for the moment, her insolent,
lazy boyfriend in Chicago.*

Stefan's hands tightened on the old steering wheel as he
heard his snarl. With long dirty hair and baggy pants,
Louie had already started asking for handouts from Stefan.
Louie had made it clear that he would not lower himself
to work in the renowned Donatien Restaurants. Estelle was
like her mother at that age: innocent and trusting, and she
did not notice Louie's gaze stripping other girls, or his
flirtation. Stefan recognized the look of lust, though he had
been celibate since the death of his wife ten years ago.

Stefan rolled his taut shoulders as he parked in front of
Granger's Wallpaper and Paint store. He had the summer
until his daughter went back to college; Louie was certain
to be unfaithful and Estelle would be protected.

He stepped from the pickup, and glanced down at his
unfamiliar clothing—jeans, a T-shirt and worn jogging
shoes. At this time of day in Chicago, he would be dressed
in a suit, busy in his office. Later on, he would dismiss his
jacket and vest and roll up his sleeves, put on an apron
and enjoy cooking in a Donatien kitchen. He couldn't wait
for the fresh herb starts that he had ordered to arrive; soon
only the best fresh farm eggs, milk and butter would go
into his omelettes, a dash of chopped chives, a sprinkle
of—

Stefan inhaled the fresh morning air, studied the small
neat town with its shops opening for customers. His
mother and daughter weren't the only ones looking forward to life in Waterville; he planned to enjoy puttering
on the farm. He smiled, enjoying the sunshine. His women
were happy, nestling into the farmhouse, decorating it, and
in his pocket were the paint samples his mother had chosen
on her two-mile bicycle ride to town. Busy with the
plumbing, Stefan had enjoyed exploring the tools the

Smiths had left behind. A man who had never had a vacation, he intended to relax in this interlude while Estelle came to her senses. Life was good...without Louie.

He entered the busy paint store, prepared to wait his turn as other customers milled around the cash register. A tall woman, wearing a baseball cap with her auburn ponytail thrust through the hole at the back, glanced at him. She hefted a gallon of paint onto the counter, slapped two wooden paint stirrers on it, rang up the bill and chatted with the customer. When the burly farmer, dressed in bib overalls, rambled out of the store, the woman scowled at Stefan. Clearly in charge of the store, the woman behind the counter wore a T-shirt that said Waterville Tigers. She was possibly in her early thirties, with soaring eyebrows, clear blue eyes, a bit of a nose and a generous mouth. Freckles covered every centimeter of her fair skin. She tapped costs into the cash register for more paint and nodded at Stefan, indicating the gallons of paint on the counter. He shook his head, not understanding her needs. With a doomed look up at the ceiling, the woman grabbed one gallon and tucked it under her arm. She eased the other into her free arm and tromped out of the store, following the elderly woman.

Stefan noted and appreciated the length of the younger woman's legs, the cutoff shorts cupping a trim, swaying bottom. The wooden paint stirrer sticks in her back pocket enhanced the movement. He was surprised that he had tilted his head to better appreciate that little feminine jiggle of flesh at her backside. She walked back into the store, strode to him and shook her head as Stefan noted the slant of her eyes, those strong cheekbones gleaming in the overhead light. The drop of cobalt-blue paint on her cheeks matched the color of her eyes as they burned up at him. The shadows beneath her eyes said she had missed sleep and the area around her mouth was pale, demonstrating her strain.

She reached to tug away the two bits of toilet paper on his jaw. He had been unwise to shave after the furious argument with his daughter; the small cuts marked his broken promise to remain calm. A man who spared little time on women of moods, except his daughter and his mother, Stefan firmed his lips. He was determined not to let this woman ruin his day. Then she said, ''I know you can't talk—you're the cousin that Ned Whitehouse told me needed work. I told him to have you turn up and work, helping me. Well, that's what you should be doing—helping. You could have carried out that paint for Mrs. Mariah. Come on. Follow me.''

She moved through the displays of paint and carpeting toward the back room, behind the checkout counter. Unused to taking orders, Stefan stood still and crossed his arms.

The woman continued talking—''I want you to clean up the storeroom and then fix that back door—it's almost coming off the hinges. One good yank and hell-o—free paint for everyone. Not that anyone in Waterville steals, but a good business should have a good back door, don't you agree?''

Stefan thought of the alarm systems and locks he'd required on all Donatien restaurant back doors, ones made of sturdy metal, and nodded.

When she noted that he had not followed her, she turned and those arching fine eyebrows drew into a stern frown. She walked back to him, her hands on her hips. Stefan tried not to notice the T-shirt that had tightened across her breasts. They were just the size of medium cooking apples, not too big or too small, but just perfect.

Stefan frowned, unprepared for the turn of his thoughts.

He did not usually compare women to his favorite pastimes—choosing fine foods, preparing and enjoying them.

In his mind, he compared her height to his, how she would fit against him. The top of her head would just come to his chin. Those breasts would press against his chest and those long legs would—

She crossed her arms and tapped her running shoe on the floor. "I know you can hear. Ned told me so. He also said that sometimes you can be stubborn as his mules. Well, today isn't one of them, got that? I haven't got time for this, so get your butt in gear and start helping me. Saturdays are usually busy, but nothing like spring and fall. I've been running shorthanded during the busiest season of the year and everyone wants to paint every room in the kingdom. Not that I'm objecting to the sales, which aren't good except for spring and fall, but *I could use some help*," she stated meaningfully.

Then shaking her head, she said very carefully as if to make him understand better, "Okay. I'll up the hourly wage and pay overtime. If you don't help me, I don't know what I'll do."

She placed her hands on her ball cap as if holding her head together. Her hands were feminine, yet strong, with short nails spotted with paint. Stefan tried not to smile; if he were in a business argument with power titans, he would have known that he had the upper hand at her concession. On the other hand, he was enjoying the masquerade—no one had ever mistaken him for a laborer. The scenario into which he had dropped amused him. Clearly this woman was under pressure and it appealed to him to rescue her. He decided not to speak, because his slight accent would surely mark him as the newcomer in Waterville. He wondered what it would be like, not to be Stefan Donatien, powerful restaurateur, rather to be an ordinary workman for a day. He had found his "cave" away from the brooding women he loved.

She looked up at him. "My name is Rose and yours is Bruce, and we'll get along fine, if you just do what I tell you to do. It's Saturday and the whole town is set to buy paint, wallpaper and carpet and I need you. Not that I don't appreciate the business. I'll even buy lunch—hot dogs and potato salad with lemonade from Danny's Café, and all the coffee you can drink... Just don't use my cup. Lyle and Joe are out laying carpet, but you can meet them later. Everyone here works part-time, but me. Did you come to work or not?"

Stefan nodded slowly, though her choice of food turned his stomach, and in seconds they were in the back room where she was pointing and ordering like a general. "Sturdy up those shelves, separate the paints—oil and latex based...interior and exterior—fix the back door, and if I call you, come up front. Ned said you had your own pickup and could deliver and you may have to. I'll draw a map for you, but just don't go anywhere. Don't leave me. I've got enough problems with Dad."

He wondered about "Dad" as she turned and hurried into a small cluttered office. The bell over the store's front door jingled and she hurried to help the customer who had just entered.

Rose plopped into her desk chair, slipped her foot out of her worn running shoe and rubbed it. She was too tired from processing the store invoices until midnight, then going home to heaps of laundry. She'd missed her early-morning run, tossing her pillow over her alarm. But at seven o'clock she was making her father the bacon and egg breakfast he liked and by eight, she had opened the store. Rose frowned slightly; Maury rarely came to work,

even on the busiest days. Her father hadn't stopped mourning his runaway wife and now a whiskey bottle came too
readily to his hand. He'd taught Rose the business and
lately he almost never asked about it. He was slipping
away from her and life, spending long hours staring out
from the house porch at the rose garden his wife had loved.

Maxine Granger had not loved her family enough to stay
and raise her daughter, or to deny the passing trucker. He
offered her excitement and in time, the world, and Maxine
hadn't hesitated.

When she was ten, Rose had come home from school
to find her father crying, Maxine's goodbye note in his
hand. For a few years, there were hurried postcards from
all over the world and then nothing. It had taken Rose
years to understand that she wasn't the reason why her
mother left in that big diesel truck and why her father's
heart remained broken. As a child, she'd sat for hours at
her mother's vanity table, littered with polishes, creams
and an expensive brush for her blond hair. Rose had tried
to forget the pain, but she couldn't. Instead she pasted that
heartbreak into a locked chest marked The Past and threw
herself into helping her father at the store and at home. In
her young mind, when the ache came upon her, she raised
her arms to the moon and asked for faeries to love and
cherish her. It eased Rose-the-child to fantasize she was
being held and kissed and loved by the whimsical creatures
who would never leave her alone. Then, at times, the pain
curled around her and sucked her back, but she fought her
way out by keeping busy and thinking of the faeries that
waited for her.

She was thirty-seven now, and twelve years ago her
mother had passed away in a flaming truck wreck on the
Interstate. Her trucker-lover had sent Rose what little was
left of Maxine Granger's life. The shoe box of trinkets

included a picture of six-year-old Rose, just missing her front tooth.

Rose had little illusions about her chances for a one-and-only love. Back in the days when she believed in romance and happily-ever-after, Rose had thought her future husband and children would fill her father's aching heart. But love hadn't come to her, and she'd settled into the routine of living with her father, tending him, in the house she'd grown up in.

She rubbed the bruise on her thigh, the result of swinging a paint can from the counter to the floor. Ned's cousin had been working for an hour in the back room, straightening the gallon and pint cans on the floor. Now he was hefting the odd remnants of carpeting to stand along one side of the wall. He'd towered over her five-foot ten, looking all dark and scowling. There was an arrogance she couldn't place, just that tilt of his head, that black waving hair gleaming and neatly combed. His deep brown eyes were the color of her father's whiskey, narrowing and darkening as she talked to him. That line between his black brows and the grooves beside his mouth had deepened as if he didn't like taking orders—or smiling. His jaw had tensed, the muscle running along it contracting.

She frowned, glancing at him as he easily lifted a box of old carpet samples up to his shoulder—a very broad shoulder. Ned was right; his cousin was ''strong as an ox and a bit moody.'' He seemed to bristle each time she gave him a task, those whiskey-brown eyes narrowing on her, his jaw tensing.

Then Rose saw Henry, who she had held down and kissed when they were both in the fourth grade. When she'd shared her faerie whimsy with him, he'd laughed, later apologized. He understood Rose's pain and through the years had become a good friend.

She hurried toward the adult Henry, stood on tiptoe and kissed his cheek. In turn, he reached to turn her ball cap around, tugging it down on her head. She grinned up at him, a longtime friend and an ex-fiancé, now married to Shirley MacNeil. Rose could always depend on Henry to make her feel better—good old dependable Henry. "New man?" Henry asked as he handed her Shirley's paint list.

"Bruce. Ned's cousin. He's only helping out during the spring decorating season. He's got a surly attitude and if that doesn't stop, he's out of here."

"Maybe he doesn't like bossy women. Try a little patience," Henry offered with a warm, familiar smile.

"No time. Dad didn't place the orders or check the invoices and now I've got to do it."

"Is he feeling poorly?" Henry asked in his kind way. Everyone in Waterville knew that Maury Granger's visits to the liquor store were becoming more frequent.

"Sure," Rose returned curtly. Instead of the usual truck delivery of paints and orders, she'd had to borrow a truck and drive one hundred miles to a manufacturer, pay over price and drive home, unloading the truck herself last Sunday. This Sunday she intended to pamper herself and firmly deal with Maury. He was a good man, but he was sinking deeper into darkness.

By noon, the new handyman had fixed the back door and was straightening the front of the store. He seemed happy until she called him into the back room for lunch, takeout food from Danny's Café, hot dogs and potato salad. With her feet propped up on the gallons of uncolored paint, and balancing her food on her stomach, she frowned as he prodded the wiener with his finger and sniffed at the bun. He scowled at the food, which nettled Rose, but then she badly needed his help and couldn't risk offending him over hot dogs. He frowned when he sipped at the coffee she'd brewed early that morning. Rose inhaled slowly and pushed her temper down; maybe Henry was right, maybe she needed to try a little kindness. "So, Bruce, do you think you might want to move up to mixing paint? It's a matter of checking the color number chart, measuring the pigment and mixing it into the uncolored gallons."

He nodded slowly, considering her with those unreadable brown eyes. Just then Larry Hershall strolled into the store, peered over a carpet display and sighted her in the back room. She waved him toward her. "How's it going, Larry?" she asked her former fiancé.

Larry nodded and grinned. "Mary Lou wants me to see that wallpaper sample she picked out for the nursery."

"Sure. Meet Bruce. He's helping me out today. He's about to move up to mixing paint."

Larry reached to shake the workman's hand and nodded. "Glad to meet you."

Ned's cousin nodded, his dark eyes following Rose and Larry as they moved to the front of the store. As comfortable with Larry as she would be with the brother she never had, Rose showed him the wallpaper sample. Standing beside him, she placed her arm on his shoulder, leaning slightly against his strength for just one moment in a hectic, tiring day.

When she returned to the back room, Ned's cousin was pouring the rest of the coffee down the paint-stained sink. His food remained untouched on the rough plank picnic table. Rose was starved, and disliking waste, asked, "Going to eat this?"

When he shook his head, she slathered mustard, relish and ketchup onto the hot dog. Rose had balanced a household budget from an early age and did not waste food.

"Yummy," she said when he watched her devour the hot dog.

She didn't want to ask about his disdainful expression. He was a good workman and she desperately needed him. If she could manage to establish a basic relationship with him, he might stay to help her. "So, Bruce. Let's put in a hard day here—I'll move you up to mixing paint—and then if you'd like, you can come fishing with my dad and me. Crappie start biting at the lake just after supper. You might even catch a bass. What do you say?"

He nodded slowly just as the bell over the front door jingled. The delightful Frenchwoman who had come in the previous day smiled warmly over the displays. Rose, followed closely by her new handyman, went to help the customer.

"Ma chérie," Yvette Donatien said smoothly with that enticing accent. Her blond-and-gray hair softly framed an exquisite face, shaded by a floppy straw hat. A simple cotton dress swirled around Yvette's rounded body, emphasizing her femininity just like the spring daisies tucked into her hat ribbon. She carried a shopping basket made of oak strips. The basket had been made locally by Linda Brooks and fit perfectly into the metal one on Yvette's bicycle. Rose had instantly liked the charming Frenchwoman with her ready smile and humor.

Yvette smiled warmly at the man behind Rose, and then momentarily a puzzled expression crossed her face. Tracing Yvette's stare, Rose looked up swiftly to see the handyman stroking his index finger across his raised brows. His expression was bland and innocent. "Oh, that's Bruce," Rose said. "He's new. He's a good worker and he's about to graduate to paint mixing."

"I see," Yvette said, glancing at the man again and then back at Rose. Her blue eyes twinkled as she smiled

warmly. "I stopped by to say how much I enjoyed our
visit yesterday. My son will be stopping by soon. I hope
you like him. He can be very formal and arrogant at times,
perhaps a little old-world in his ways—stuffy, if you will.
But he is a good boy. He tries very hard to be a good
papa, though he sometimes does not understand women.
I'll be going now. I'm so enjoying your delightful community."

Yvette frowned slightly at the man behind Rose, who
sensed the restlessness in him. She hoped that he wouldn't
show his poor manners to a potentially good customer and
a woman she liked immediately. After Yvette exited the
store, Rose shot an elbow back into her employee's hard
stomach. He grunted and when she turned, his scowl was
fierce upon her. "Listen, you," she said. "You're going
to have to put on a nice face for customers. It may be hard,
but try. I could almost feel you bristling behind me. I've
already heard that Stefan Donatien is a hard case, but his
mother is very nice and I like her."

She ignored the flaring of his nostrils, the tightening of
his mouth. A woman who related easily to men, she wasn't
intimidated. Perhaps the handyman had been bruised by
life, or had a serious health problem. She was very good
at getting men to relate to her; once she understood his
problem, perhaps they could develop a smooth working
relationship. She decided to push right past his bad mood
before she fired a man she badly needed. "Are you going
fishing with us tonight, or not?"

He nodded grimly, his big body rigid. Waves of temper
poured off him, and she had no time for dealing with that.
"Well, let's start you on paint mixing then. It's all done
by formula. Here's the chart of the amounts of dry powder
that you mix into the basic formula. You use this—" she
held up a rubber mallet "—to close it and shake—" She

indicated a machine. ''Make certain you seal it and clamp it good, because it's a big mess for you to clean up, if you don't. Oh, stop sulking and scowling. You'll scare away my customers. You really need to lighten up, Bruce.''

By three o'clock, Rose craved a refreshing nap that she wasn't going to get. Business was really good, and her new handyman was efficient at mixing paint. Though he didn't speak, he seemed to be making an effort to be charming, smiling at the customers. He wasn't that hard looking when he smiled and the women seemed to like him, discussing their decorator plans with him and considering his pointing finger on the samples. In fact, he had made several good sales, selling the carpet remnants from past years. He carried purchases out for customers and Rose decided to trust him with making a delivery to Ella Parsons. ''Hey, Bruce. Here's the map to Ella Parsons. She lives a distance out in the country, so try to help her with whatever she needs doing and get back here to help me close up, okay?''

He took the map she had drawn, folded it neatly and slid it into his back pocket. He crossed his arms and considered her intently. His dark gaze roamed her face, her throat and slowly moved down her body. That close examination caused Rose to shiver. Ned's cousin didn't need words to express a male attraction to her. She flipped over the thought; perhaps he was just shy and looking for a friend. She knew how to be a man's friend, if not his love.

In the next minute, a rush of customers consumed her. Her new employee efficiently mixed paint and when the rush slowed, loaded Granger's delivery truck. Alone and tending the customers, Rose worked furiously. During spring and fall seasonal rushes, every minute counted.

Just minutes from closing time, a thin, clean, but poorly dressed young man entered the store. When she went to help him, he signed with his hands. Not understanding his meaning, Rose offered him a pad and pencil.

"I'm Bruce Long, Ned's cousin," he wrote. "Woke up feeling bad. Had car trouble. Sorry to be late."

Rose stood absolutely still, her mind replaying the day's scenarios. Whoever the stranger was who had worked all day, he wasn't Bruce. "Come back early Monday, okay?" she asked, hurriedly pushing him out of the door.

She rushed to the telephone beside the cash register and dialed Ella Parsons. The man she had mistaken for Bruce Long could be a murderer, a thief, and she'd sent him directly to a dear elderly woman. Fear tore through Rose as she worried about Ella's safety. "Ella? Did you get your delivery?"

"I did, dear. Everything is in perfect order, and so is that nice Mr. Donatien. We had the nicest chat. He cooked a lovely dinner for Edward and me, and we dined together. He's coming back with his mother in the morning for fresh eggs and milk. She wants some good cream cows and my Edward is going to help find someone with cows to spare. I love a man who treats his mother well like Mr. Donatien. He clearly loves her and his daughter. Not every man would give up a fancy business office and a secretary waiting on his every command to give his family the country life they want. He's on his way back to your store now, I think. Lovely man, Mr. Donatien."

"Oh, he is, is he?" Rose asked very slowly and gripped the counter until her fingers ached. She had a few things to say to Stefan Donatien, and none of them were sweet.

Two

Stefan parked the delivery truck in the lot beside Granger's store. He carefully retrieved the two pink plastic flamingos from the passenger side of the truck. He held the yard ornaments carefully, a welcome gift from Ella Parsons, who said that everyone who was anyone in Waterville had pink flamingos in their yards. At five o'clock, the store would soon be closing, and he had had an interesting, stress-relieving day. He'd put the blistering argument with Estelle back into perspective—she was becoming her own person and it was normal girl-to-woman development to test herself against life—and her father. He loved her and she loved him, and once they were through this Louie-phase, life would be much simpler.

His mother was delighted with Waterville. The small town reminded her of her youth in France. The farm was as quaint as the town, the milk cows perfect for the cheese and butter Yvette longed to make. She loved feeding her baby chicks and planning her vegetable garden. In the pasture next to his farm, Estelle was already riding horses with a girl her age.

His women also loved the contents of the old farmhouse. It was filled with ordinary, mismatched furniture, far from that of Stefan's penthouse. The Smiths were ready to travel full-time in their camper and didn't want the old furniture that so enchanted Stefan's mother and daughter.

He smiled, cruising along in the mellow and happy lane, certain the Donatiens' lives would settle happily.

Sunlight filtered through the trees lining the street and danced along the flower beds resting on the sidewalk in front of the stores. Next door, the barber was just locking his front door. Waterville was quiet and peaceful and perfect, the spit and whittle men's bench vacated until Monday.

Stefan entered the front of the store with a sense of well-being. Around the towering stack of gallon paint cans, he spotted an angry Rose. She stalked right toward him, and on her way, reached for a softball from the counter and hurled it at him. He caught it in one hand, while protectively cradling the pink flamingos with the other arm. She came to stand in front of him, her hands braced on her waist, her legs apart as if readying for a fight. Her blue eyes lasered at him, and her freckles seemed to shift on her face as if waiting to attack him. In his good mood, Stefan smiled slightly at the thought of a ''Rose'' freckle attack. He realized instantly that humor had not been a part of his life for some time.

''You're grinning. Some big joke, huh? *You are not Bruce Long,*'' Rose stated tightly.

Stefan turned the Open sign to Closed. He wanted this conversation to be private. Rose looked as if she might erupt. ''I did not say that I was.''

''You cooked for Ella…put wine in her spaghetti sauce. You gave her tips on the presentation of green beans, not snapped, but whole…. Everyone here snaps green beans. They usually cook green beans with bacon, and maybe onion instead of steaming them…sometimes with new potatoes. You'll have everyone canning their June beans upright in the jars…and every once in a while, I get to sit on someone's front porch and snap beans. I enjoy that— *and you're messing with Waterville tradition.*''

''The presentation of the meal is ultimate. We dined together. The Parsons are quite charming, and I was quite hungry—my stomach could not bear your infamous hot dogs,'' Stefan returned, watching in fascination as Rose tore the rubber band confining her ponytail away. A sleek curtain of burnished reddish brown hair fell to her shoulders. He longed to crush it in his hands, to lift it to the sunlight and to study the fascinating color and texture. It would feel like silk, alive with warmth from Rose. He breathed unsteadily as an image flashed through his mind—that of Rose's hair dragging along his bare skin, the sensual sweep of the rich reddish-brown strands across his cheek.

Stefan held still, shocked by the turn of his thoughts; he had not been so susceptible since he was in his teens. Perhaps it was spring, the flowers, the lack of Louie— ''Hello, Rose,'' he said gently, loving the sound on his tongue.

She reminded him of a flower, as fresh as dewdrops glistening in the dawn.

''You've got an accent. That's why you didn't talk. And I fell for it,'' Rose-the-flower stated darkly. ''Very funny.''

He looked down at the check she'd thrust into his hand. ''Get out,'' she said tightly. ''I know you own a chain of French restaurants and that check isn't even the price of a meal in one of them. But I owe you for the work and I'm paying up.''

For an instant, Stefan tensed. No one spoke to him in that tone. He focused on Rose and said slowly, ''Does that mean that the invitation to go fishing with you at the lake is off?''

''You knew that at the time—'' she began hotly.

''So you are a woman who takes back what she has offered,'' he said, watching her closely. Ella had briefly informed him of Rose's unfortunate love life—engaged three times and never married—and of her dedication to a father who was slowly drinking more. Stefan wanted to hold Rose close and protect her, this bit of a woman, all sleek and soft and exciting. His verbal nudge was intended to seal his time with her at the lake. He wanted to know more about her, this woman who fought so valiantly against odds, who loved so deeply. He wanted to see her eat one wholesome meal and relax. He wanted to place his hands on those taut, overworked, feminine muscles and give them ease. He wanted to capture that capable feminine hand, turn it and press a kiss into her palm. He wanted to cup that curved bottom in both hands. He wanted to taste the flavor of her breasts, those perfect, applelike breasts.

She seemed so natural and totally unaware of her appeal, unlike the women in his experience. Women who seemed interested in him usually wanted his checkbook, not himself. He'd watched Rose tend her customers. She did not hide her emotions. She genuinely liked most of them, that brilliant smile flashing at them, or she touched them. Once she'd waited on a customer, her face taut and grim, all her walls were up and Stefan knew she did not like the man.

Now, the sunlight shafted through the store's windows

and tipped her dark brown eyelashes in fire. An answering flame danced in his heart, in his loins.

Ten years of abstinence was far too long, he decided instantly, and wondered if the flush upon her face would be the same after they made love. He longed to see her soft and drowsy beneath him. Somehow, his instincts told him that he had found a woman to enjoy and treasure; with her, he could find peace.

"I don't like being made a fool of," Rose shot at him angrily, shredding his vision of peace and pleasure.

"Ah, so then, you retreat from the battle," he nudged again. "You fear you might like me. You fear that I might catch more fish than you. You fear that your father will like me, too."

Her lips parted and she blinked up at him, her expression blank. "You haven't talked all day and now you're saying too much. Don't you get it? I'm mad at you."

He shrugged, determined to have his way. "So you do retreat. I have won."

Those blue eyes widened and blinked again. "Won what?"

"The game. You are afraid. You retreat. I win. Simple."

She shook her head and the reddish hues in her hair caught the overhead light. "You wouldn't like fishing at the lake. Chiggers, mosquitoes, every biting insect possible," she explained. "When the flies bite here, it hurts. The johnboat isn't a yacht—it's a chopped-off metal boat—and the crappie are sporting, but they aren't swordfish, Mr. Donatien."

"It sounds delightful," he said, watching that faint sunlight stroke her cheek and wondering if the freckle pattern continued over her body. He went a little light-headed thinking about those long, athletic limbs, those perfect apple-shaped breasts, the way she took fire. Rose Granger was a passionate woman for certain, and just watching her move provoked an excitement in his body that he hadn't expected.

She inhaled slowly, balled her fists at her sides, and frowned up at him. "Be at the north end of the lake at six-thirty. You'll have to find the johnboat tied to the dock. I've got to pick up Dad."

"I must get the paint my mother wishes."

"Take care of your own order. Just leave the cash on the counter, or leave your check and I'll send the change to you," Rose said, moving restlessly behind the counter and avoiding his gaze.

She was sweet and shy of him, Stefan realized as she hurried out the back door. He enjoyed that little jiggle of soft flesh below her shorts' ragged hem; he traced her long legs down to the back of her knees. He closed his eyes, riveted by the need to kiss her there, where she seemed most vulnerable and virginal.

In a good mood, because he would spend time with an enchanting woman later, Stefan kissed one of the flamingos' plastic beaks. He frowned into the bird's vacant yellow eyes. Was he nervous? His first attraction to a woman, since his wife? But, of course, and he was so hungry for the taste of that lush, sassy mouth—

Carrying her tackle box and fishing pole, Rose tromped from her pickup, across the lush grass of the lake's bank. She'd tried desperately to rouse her sleeping father and had failed. She'd debated leaving Stefan—the wealthy, continental businessman she'd ordered around all day—to the mosquitoes and biting red chiggers. But her competitive streak, which allowed her to be captain of the mixed softball team, was revved. Nothing could have kept her from watching him itch—payback for deceiving her all day.

Her thoughts slapped against her in rhythm to the sound of her plastic thongs. She glanced at the slash of scarlet, a male cardinal bird in the oak trees. *If he had only spoken just one word, she would have known who he was—his deep enchanting accent would have marked him as the newcomer...though he didn't seem as cold as Harry at the gas station had inferred.*

She pushed away the memory of Stefan's smile at the pink flamingos. It was excited, almost as if he were a boy, excited at winning trophies.

Stefan was sitting on the dock, his pole already in the water, the shadows and sunlight flowing over his body, the water sparkling beyond him. At around six-feet four inches he could intimidate with that dark scowl, but not her. Her thongs clumped as she walked out onto the dock, studied the metal johnboat and decided she didn't want to baby the worn motor into life. She slung her backpack—filled with cola, a peanut butter sandwich and insect repellent—down to the worn boards of the dock. Out in the glimmering still water, a big mouth bass surged up for a juicy water bug, reminding Rose of how she had taken Stefan's challenge. She glanced at the expert way Stefan cast into the lake's dead timber, the perfect place for a ''crappie bed.'' It was her private place. ''Dad couldn't come. We can fish here,'' she said. ''You stay on your side of the dock, and I'll stay on mine. You'd better have your fishing license. I like your mother. I don't like you.''

His hair was damp, curling at his nape and that all-man soap smell curled erotically around her. The clean T-shirt tightened across his shoulders as he patted the billfold in his back pocket. ''I have a license.... So you have had a bad day, and you wish to take it out on me, right?'' he asked.

Rose slipped off her thongs, plopped down on the dock and dangled her legs over the side as Stefan was doing. She wouldn't be waylaid by that sexy, intimate accent. She opened her tackle box and selected just the right fishing ''jig,'' a plastic lure to entice crappie. Only meeting Stefan's challenge had kept her from falling facedown on her bed and sleeping through Sunday. She was *not* a woman who offered and then took back her invitation. She cast, propped the handle of her pole into the slot between the boards and took out her insect repellent, rubbing it on her arms and legs. She sniffed lightly and recognized the slight tang of citronella, also an insect deterrent, coming from Stefan. He would not be leaving her dock soon. ''Can we just be quiet?'' she asked. ''I've looked forward to this all week.''

For the next half hour, she felt the old dock tremble slightly as Stefan cast into her favorite fishing hole. The crappie responded to his lure, flip-flopping in the water as he reeled them in and released them. She refused to ask what he was using for bait, because nothing was nibbling at her line. He held up one and asked, ''How do you prepare crappie?''

She looked over her shoulder and wished she hadn't. The fish was Old George, a legendary giant of a crappie, who had escaped her hook. ''You wait until you get a 'mess' and then fillet, score, bread in flour and cornmeal and fry. Or you might dip them in egg or beer batter...serve with wilted lettuce... But I'd throw that one back, he's too small,'' she lied, because she wanted Old George on her dinner table. ''Did you enjoy yourself today, your little masquerade?''

He unhooked Old George and tossed him back into the

lake. Stefan dipped his hands in the lake and washed them as would an experienced fisherman. He looked over his shoulder at her and grinned. It was a devastating, boyish grin that took her breath away. "I learned so much."

Rose turned back and promptly missed the dip of her red bobber in the water as a fish nibbled on her lure. It was difficult to concentrate when Stefan spread his blanket, sat upon it and began opening the basket he had brought. "My mother likes you, too. She was excited that I had a date with you and packed this meal for us."

Rose pivoted to him, temper flashing. "This isn't a date, Mr. Donatien." She leveled her words at him, not wanting him to get any flashy, upscale ideas about a country girl.

"But I am with a very fascinating woman and I am enjoying myself. Surely that is a date." He began unpacking, carefully placing a wine bottle that looked very costly, onto the blanket. He opened the bottle with a flourish and poured the wine into two very expensive-looking stemmed glasses. He unwrapped cheese and studied it. "My mother thinks she will make cheese here. She is happy and reliving her young life on a French farm, I think. My daughter is...happy in one way, not so in another."

Rose watched as he sliced the cheese and a very-hard looking sausage, placing crusty bread rolls beside it. She couldn't resist the temptation to ask, "Why isn't your daughter happy?"

He shrugged a broad shoulder and looked out at the peaceful lake. His features were unreadable. "She is happy to be here. She is not happy with me. It is a hard passage from the girl to the woman. A boy I do not like wants her."

Rose stared at him; the unlikely, worldly Donatiens moving to Waterville suddenly made sense. "You maneuvered this whole move to Waterville, didn't you? Just to get her away from—''

Stefan scowled and handed her one filled wineglass. ''From Louie The Freeloader. Estelle wished to live in an average, small town and I merely arranged her wishes. Perhaps I was ready for a change, too. My mother had been speaking of her homeland and selfishly, I wished to keep my family—what there is of it—together. Waterville was selected after very thorough research. We will spend the summer here. The farm was a compromise to make them both happy. It had been up on the market since the Smiths decided to see the West in their camper. There is a college some miles away, which might suit Estelle's needs, if she wishes to transfer.''

''I hate to tell you this, Pops, but there are hot-blooded boys here in Waterville, too.'' Rose sipped the wine and studied him. ''You left everything to prevent Louie and Estelle from—''

His scowl deepened. ''They have not consummated. I would know.''

''Maybe they are in love,'' she suggested, fascinated by his absolute confidence. ''How would you know?''

''I am her father,'' he said roughly with an arrogant tilt to his head, that accent more distinct. ''You think I do not know my own daughter? That I have been so absorbed in business that I would not recognize the change?''

Though she'd been angry with him, and had found his tender spot, Rose recognized the troubled road between father and daughter. She sympathized with both of them. ''I was engaged about that age,'' she said gently.

''But it did not last,'' he prompted as another bass rolled in the lake, turning a silver side in the dark, shadowy water. ''That is why you and I are here together. A good husband would have kept you happy.''

The crickets and frogs chirped as Rose shook her head. She munched on the crusty bread Stefan had torn apart and handed to her and thought about how romance wasn't for her.

"What happened?" Stefan asked softly.

A flat-shelled water turtle crawled up onto a log, half sunken in the still water, and looked at the humans. Stefan was just passing through her life; it was a moment in time that meant nothing, she told herself. There was no reason not to share with him something that happened long ago. "It seemed only natural to marry Henry. We were lifetime friends and everyone else was getting married at the time. It's contagious, you know. He came into the store today and got paint. Henry is like a comfortable old shoe, all broken in and fitting just right. We did the engagement party thing, but as the wedding date came closer, neither one of us wanted to go through with it. Not really. We sort of got caught up in the engagement fun, the party and excitement. But he wasn't happy and I knew it, because I wasn't, either. So I pinned him down one night—sat on him—and we had an honest chat. He married my best friend, Shirley MacNeil. They've got two great kids...boys. They're hoping for a girl next time. I am god-mother to their children, and others in Waterville. I guess that's as close as I'm going to get to motherhood."

Stefan's dark brows rose. "The man you hugged so in-timately? You remain friends with him?"

"Sure. No hard feelings. It just wasn't right between us. I can always count on Henry to help me in a tight spot." She shrugged and munched on the cheese and meat he handed her.

"Good old Henry, right?" Stefan said tightly as he re-filled the wineglass she had just emptied. "Who was the man you leaned against as if you trusted him?"

She eyed Stefan, considering him. They were strangers sharing a quiet moment on a lovely, peaceful evening. The wine was relaxing her after a hard week of work. "I don't know why I shouldn't tell you, everyone else knows. Waterville's quiet country life will bore you soon enough and you'll be back to the city's society set soon. That was Larry. We were engaged for a time. He rented a motel room away from Waterville for our first—" She raised her wineglass, toasting the moment when neither could become aroused enough to make love. "Happening. It didn't happen. End of story. He and Mary Lou are expecting their first baby. Everything turned out fine."

Stefan's dark eyes cruised the body she had just spread full-length upon his blanket. He lay down, sharing the blanket, the food between them. He propped his head in one hand and placed a bit of cheese into her mouth with the other. His eyes darkened as she ate. He asked, "Why didn't it happen?"

"I laughed when I saw him naked for the first time. And my bony mystique seemed pretty funny to him, too. Our batteries just weren't charged. We decided we were better suited to be friends than lovers. We used to come here, my friends and I, when we were young. We used to tell ghost stories and—I don't know why, but the attraction just wasn't there, not enough to…to do it, or to marry. Then there was Mike. He hadn't been in town very long when we started dating. He was a super pitcher on the team. He was a good mechanic—could fix anything. We got engaged and then one night, I caught him tuning some-one else's engine and he left town soon after…. I'm sorry about your wife. Your mother said you loved her deeply."

"I still do. Claire will always be a part of my life. She lives in my daughter. She had the same straight black hair."

Rose studied Stefan's broad, blunt cheekbones, that square chin, and wondered about his wife. What kind of woman could take his heart? A gentle woman? Feminine and pretty? A quiet woman, who understood? A fascinating woman, full of life? A corporate wife, all glossy and perfect? Or was she a woman like Rose's mother—who loved and captivated every man and left them mourning her as she moved on? "Estelle will have to make up her own mind, you know. You can't protect her from life forever."

"Who protects you?" he asked softly and ran a finger slowly down her cheek.

Her skin heated at the touch and she shifted away, uneasy with a man who seemed too intimate, too soon, too foreign, too unique, too exciting—and just "too." She looked at the clouds floating gently across the sky, just as her life seemed to be doing. "I'm way, way past that age."

"So old." Humor hovered in Stefan's deep voice.

"Well, let's just say I've settled in for the long run. No surprises, no problems—"

She stared up at the man leaning over her, looking deeply, intimately into her eyes. "What? Is something wrong?"

"You have given up on life as an appealing, vital woman. You are preparing for your rocking chair and shawl. Are you not aware of how enticing you are?"

She sucked in air when she realized she'd stopped breathing. Men usually thought of her as a good friend. Stefan's sultry gaze seemed to devour her mouth as if he wanted to kiss her. The quiver passing through her body, the raised hairs on the back of her neck, startled her.

"Are you making a pass at me, bud?" she asked carefully, because men never flirted with her. She'd added the "bud" to keep him at a distance.

His smile was slow and warming and mind-blowing. It was definitely not a good-buddy smile. ''So blunt. I will have to adjust to your frank style of conversation. It has been a while, and perhaps I am out of practice at making my intentions known.''

Then he placed his hands on either side of her head, studied the shape of her mouth beneath his and lowered his head. The kiss was that of a man who knew what he wanted and was confident he could obtain it. The kiss felt like a possession, a tantalizing gift and a choice. His lips were firm, yet light against hers, seeking more than demanding, exploring the shape and taste of her as if he had all the time in the world. Rose mentally rummaged for her resistance and failed. She felt herself drift away in the summer evening, tethered only by the temptation of his mouth. The dock shook...or was it her?

When he lifted his head, his eyes were dark and warm and yet tender. Rose slowly pushed away the sensation that she could melt into his arms and forget everything but the steamy pulsing of their bodies— She breathed carefully, studying Stefan's dark, sultry gaze. ''If...if you're looking to start something, don't.''

He stroked a strand of her hair, studying the reddish shades in the dying light. ''Why not?''

She couldn't afford to give herself again. While she had explained her love life to him as though it hadn't affected her, the pain had been terrible. Though the decisions to break the engagements were shared, she'd been left with the sense that others moved on—like her mother—while she was left alone. She did not want to open herself again for a security that wasn't there. Stefan was only passing through her life, testing her and playing his games. ''I've never been a one-night stand and I don't intend to be.''

That warm, intimate look cooled and sizzled with anger. "You think that is what I offer you?"

Rose pushed herself to her feet, gathered her backpack and tackle box and stood looking down at him. Stefan's arms were behind his head. He took up too much space on the dock, and too much of Rose's air—she was suddenly finding breathing difficult. She forced her gaze away from that wide chest and flat stomach up to his dark, sultry eyes, locking with them as he said, "You are afraid. You like to be in control of the men you take, and yourself. You fear giving away too much."

"I do not," she said harshly. How could he possibly know how she *had* to be in control, to survive, to take care of her father and herself and the business that supported them? How could he know how much she had loved a mother, who had deserted her?

He slanted her a disbelieving look. "You responded. You are a woman. You are alive."

"Oh, I hate it when you shoot out those machine-gun sentences, summing up everything to your reasoning. If you need relief, I'm not your girl." With that she hurried away to safety, to her home. Her hands shook as she shifted her pickup, and the gears protested her careless handling.

Her father continued to sleep and Rose settled in for a restless night. She tossed upon her single bed, the rosebud sheets tangling between her legs. Stefan did not kiss like other men in her experience. He kissed her as if he was imprinting her taste upon his mind, as if he needed the taste of her to carry with him. He spoke very softly, his accent curling intimately around her. She sensed an awakening within herself that wouldn't be quelled. It was a long time before she slept, the taste of Stefan's kiss—firm, sensual, tempting, hungry—dancing through her dreams.

She tried to snuggle down in her bed, and into the safety she had created in her life. But dreams of Stefan, stretched out on the dock and looking sexy, wrapped around her.

On the one morning she could sleep in, Rose smelled coffee. If her father—if Maury was tipsy and cooking, the situation could be dangerous. She pushed herself out of bed, and dressed only in briefs and the T-shirt she used for a nightgown, slowly made her way down the stairs. At the kitchen doorway, she yawned and rubbed her eyes and longed to curl up back in bed, regaining the sleep Stefan Donatien had robbed from her. "Dad? Are you okay?"

Sunlight shafted through the kitchen windows and Rose blinked. Seated at the kitchen table, her father waved an airy greeting. His face was wrapped in a towel. A basin was on the table, and Yvette Donatien was rubbing a shaving brush in Maury's old-fashioned soap mug. She eased off the towel, slathered his jaw with soapy foam and began expertly stroking a straight razor over his jaw. Dressed in another soft flowing, flower-print dress, she looked at home in the kitchen. "'*Al-lo,* Rose. You look so sleepy, *ma chérie,*" she said, her voice soft and musical. "Come, sit down. When Maury is shaved, we will eat. Come. Enjoy this beautiful morning. It will only be a moment before Stefan serves his famous *Piperade* omelet, from the South of France. We have the basket of fresh eggs from the Parsons and a few ingredients from your home, and *voilà,* my beautiful son's omelet. I think we will soon have our own cows and mushrooms from the farm's root cellar. Stefan and I were just passing by and I noticed Maury—looking so alone—in his beautiful rose garden."

"I invited them in for breakfast. I was going to cook some bacon and eggs," Maury murmured in nasal tones, because Yvette was holding his nose to shave beneath it. "I said I'd better shave first, and Yvette offered to give me an old-fashioned one with a straight razor. And sure enough I found mine in the medicine cabinet, still sharp as a knife. Couldn't pass that offer up," he said cheerfully.

Stefan turned slowly from the kitchen stove to look at Rose. She couldn't move, pinned by his narrowed gaze, as it roamed her body. Yvette continued to talk while Rose tried to find reality and slow the racing of her heart. Stefan's look said he wanted to carry her off to bed, to claim her. The stark desire written on his expression terrified Rose...because if his kiss of yesterday was any indication, she didn't stand a chance to resist him.

"Be right back," she said and turned, hurrying upstairs to dress in a short, summer shift. After one look in the mirror, she remembered Stefan's expression as his gaze traced her legs. She quickly changed to jeans and a T-shirt. Instinctively she knew that Stefan was not a man to take a "just friends" attitude with her. He was too intense, and she had to protect herself. She would manage to be civil for their parents' sake and that would be the end of Mr. Stefan Donatien, she decided firmly.

When she returned, Maury was watching Yvette in the laundry room, located just off the kitchen. Laughing gayly, she was filling the clothes washer, and Maury's expression caused Rose to stand still and stare. He seemed younger, more intense, and if Rose didn't know better— She shook her head. Her father couldn't be flirting. She blinked. Yet he was and there was that *hungry male* look at Yvette's hips as she bent over to fill the clothes dryer.

She looked up to see Stefan studying her. "You are worried," he whispered simply, quietly. "She has a good heart and does not hurt."

Then he bent to place his cheek beside hers for just that

fraction of a heartbeat. "Do not worry, your father is safe. There is no need for you to protect him. It is only friendship she offers. She has never been truly involved with another man since my father, though she likes to dance and laugh and enjoy their company."

Rose shivered, uncertain of herself, of her suddenly animated father, and of Stefan, who had just turned that slight little bit to brush his lips across hers. That light touch packed a jolt of electricity and she stepped back, frowning at him. She remembered all the times she'd reached for happiness, only to have it slap her in the face. She'd cling to the safety of approaching spinsterhood, no worrying about engagements, weddings or love that just wasn't there. "I'm just a country girl and I will not be the dessert of the day," she informed him.

But Stefan was wearing that same *hungry* expression she had seen on the face of her father. It was a look that said Stefan wasn't likely to be dismissed easily.

Three

"I thought you would be here," Stefan said as he walked onto the dock that evening. Rose was sitting in the johnboat, the rope still tied to the dock as she fished. Stefan noted that her line was in the exact place where he had caught the crappie she obviously did not want him to have. He knew the average size of crappie and his catch had been a prize. "If you are not careful, you will catch that small crappie I released last night."

Dressed in cutoffs, a T-shirt and her ball cap, she ignored him as he sat on the dock. With her legs draped over the side of the boat and her bare feet in the water, she was lovely against the evening shadows. She slowly reeled the line, causing her lure to quiver beneath the water. A bullfrog bellowed, cutting coarsely across the gentle evening sounds. Rose continued to ignore Stefan, and he settled his dinner basket on the dock. "You spoke little at breakfast. You ate little."

Rose breathed slowly and the setting sun stroked the rise and fall of her breasts. ''Breakfast—that whatever you call it—was good. You were uninvited then and you are uninvited now.''

''That was quite by accident. My mother is impulsive and friendly. She also is very soft in her heart. She wanted to stop. When you know her better, you will understand. And your father did look lonely.''

Rose turned to look at him fully. ''Well, he's not lonely now. He's at your place, painting walls with your mother. It took him an hour to get ready. He pressed a good cotton shirt and asked me how he looked. Dad hasn't cared about his looks since I don't know when. Tomorrow he's coming to work for the first time in months. He said he needed to get back 'in the flow.' He hasn't been 'in the flow' since my mother left.''

Stefan shrugged. His mother might appreciate the company and help, but companionship was her limit. His daughter was at the movies with her new girlfriend, swooning over the latest screen hero. It was good for Estelle to be with friends of her own age and for Louie to be far, far away. For the first time in ages, Stefan felt at peace. ''This is good,'' he said, meaning it as he inhaled the sweet evening air. ''And I am not playing a game, by the way.''

''Hey, guy. You're here for the summer as I understand, and you're messing in my life. You're temporary. I'm permanent. There's a difference. What do you want from me?'' Rose asked, her voice carrying huskily across the lake's distance, her expression shadowed.

Stefan reached to grip the rope tethering her boat and gently pulled her closer until he could see those magnificent blue eyes and those wonderful freckles. He wrapped his hand around her ankle and stroked it with his thumb, enjoying the feel of her flesh. "I find you attractive and enchanting and magnificently delicious."

"That's quite the line," she tossed back at him after a moment's hesitation in which she was obviously picking her way to safety. She pulled her leg away from his touch.

Stefan smiled, pushing aside the way she could nettle him, dismissing his good intentions. "You just missed a nibble."

She frowned at him and reeled in her line. Stefan appreciated the graceful cast into the crappie bed, the way her slender arms held power and confidence and beauty. He wished they were holding him tightly, that her skin was damp and soft and sweet against his own. The fading sunlight gleamed on her long, bare legs and he wished those, too, were wrapped around him. It was not easy to wait for her when his body had just awakened to his needs. "How long will it take for you to trust me?"

"You haven't got that long. I know exactly what you want and then when you have it, you'll move on. I don't intend to be one of the local delicacies you choose to sample. And if you knew me better—which you aren't going to—you'd know that I'm not delicate."

"I would guess that Mike is the reason for your opinion. You said he came into town and left. The other two fiancés were lifelong friends. Since I am new here, I am to pay for Mike and his defection, is that it?" Despite his intention to gain her trust, his anger was simmering now. He was an honest, honorable man seeking a woman he found desirable. Rose pushed at the dock and her boat floated back out onto the water, a distance away from him. Without weighing her disfavor, Stefan reached to grip the rope mooring her boat to the dock. He pulled it, bringing her back to him. She stuck out her foot, bracing it on the dock and keeping the distance between them.

"Would you care to have dinner with me?" he asked, perhaps a bit too forcefully, nettled that she could draw his anger from him. Only his daughter and his mother were allowed to see beneath the rigid control he had inherited from his father.

"What do I owe you for it?" she asked, watching him. Her tone was too cautious, as if some terrible game had been played on her, and she wasn't paying that penalty again.

The innuendo that he would expect payment for a meal he had prepared for her slapped him. When he was a child, his father had hammered into him that a man's honor and pride were everything. Stefan would not humble himself before Rose, telling her how his heart leaped when he saw her, how much he needed her warmth—how much he needed to give *her* warmth...and safety. Those wary blue eyes told him she had been badly hurt, and every step would be carefully weighed. That she did not trust him— a man who tried his best to be right and good—hurt. "Forget it," he said, stood and walked off before he said too much.

An hour later, Stefan gripped the farmhouse board and tugged it free, the extra force supplied by his temper. His mother had left a note that Maury had taken her for a private tour of the store, so that she could select her bathroom wallpaper undisturbed. Estelle was still out with her girlfriend. Left alone with his hunger for Rose—to hear her voice, to dream of her—Stefan concentrated on taking down the wall between the kitchen and the back porch. At least that wall was solid and could be dealt with, whereas Rose's walls were intangible but just as effective.

Stefan shook his head and tore away an old board, discarding it to the growing pile. In business, he knew how to act. But personal relationships had never come easily to him. His lack of experience with flirtation clearly was a disadvantage now.

Headlights lasered through the windows on the back porch and at a glance, Stefan recognized Rose's pickup. He had been wounded enough for one night, his attempt at friendship with her slapped in his face. He did not like the simmering anger, that of the man placing his honest intentions in front of the woman who enchanted *and* rejected him. He glanced at the woman coming up the stone walkway to the house, and with a shake of his head, opened the door.

She held up the picnic basket, her face pale in the light shafting from his home. "You forgot this."

He felt too vulnerable, an emotion denied the young son of steely Guy Donatien and firmly embedded in the man. He reached to take the handle of the basket. "Yes, of course. Thank you."

"You're lonely, aren't you?" she asked quietly above the chirp of the crickets. She did not release the basket to him.

Was he to be denied his pride? Did he have to explain the emptiness he felt in the odd hours when work did not fill his life and his family was not near? Who did this woman think she was, to pry so deeply into his life? "Are *you?*" The question was a reflex, a defense.

She shook her head and that fabulous mane of reddish-brown hair seemed to catch fire in the light. "You could get a carpenter team to help you with the house," she said, changing the subject.

Stefan did not want to admit how much he was looking forward to his new role away from business and the kitchen. He, too, wanted to enjoy average American rural life, a vacation away from stress and the city. "I do not need them."

"Larry could help. He and his brother and a few others—"

Stefan breathed deeply. Did she think he was incapable of simple tasks? He had helped remodelers and his father and knew basic carpentry. Did she think him incapable of everything? "I do not wish your ex-fiancé to be of assistance to me."

"You don't have to be so rigid about someone helping you. It's a neighborly thing to do. I've got time. We got off to a bad start, but I'll help you tonight and we'll be friends. I'll introduce you to Waterville's single women looking for a man. Just remember to keep it light, because you're only here for the summer, and some of them might want to get serious. I don't want to be held responsible for anyone's heartache."

Stefan clamped his lips closed. He refused to debate his choice of women, or to have her select them for him. He tugged the basket from her and turned, walking up the steps into the back porch. He placed the basket on a table, flipped open the top, gripped the Beaujolais wine he had selected especially to go with the *poulet en cocote*. He poured the wine into a glass, swirled it and downed it quickly. He eyed Rose, who was studying the stack of old boards and broken plasterboard. "You are a frustrating woman. Do you think me incapable of the smallest task? The smallest sense of responsibility? Do you think I ask every woman I see to have dinner with me?"

"Yes," she answered truthfully. "You're probably pretty available... I mean, a man who looks like you, who is very smooth and who is obviously wealthy."

She hadn't spared him, and Stefan reluctantly admitted

that certain women did want him. So far none of them had appealed. "'Very smooth,'" he repeated darkly.

"I've never trusted men who know how to look sexy and appealing, and how to touch a woman. And you're one of them."

Her words were both a compliment and a put-down. "Thank you for your honesty. So, I am not to be trusted."

"It's like the major leagues and minor leagues. You probably play in the majors, while I just don't want to get in the ball game at all."

He had finally found a woman who aroused and satisfied him intellectually and visually, and she did not want him. Stefan ripped open the zippered thermal pouch containing the chicken and vegetables, then tugged off a drumstick. He ate it without prowling through its taste as he usually did. Rose sniffed delicately, coming to peer down into the basket. "Eat," Stefan ordered, unconcerned with manners or presentation of the meal at the moment.

Rose studied his expression, then reached to pat his cheek. He gripped her wrist and eased it away from him. He could not bear to have her sympathy. "Don't."

She watched him carve the chicken and ladle the vegetables onto the plates, handing one to her. "Do you have to bristle?" she asked as she probed an artichoke heart with her fingertip.

When she reached for the wine, pouring it into a glass, her breast brushed Stefan's bare arm, electrifying his senses. He tensed and held his breath until the initial sensual jolt passed. "That's why I 'bristle,'" he said coarsely as she suddenly stepped back, a blush rising up her cheeks.

He took the finger she had used to test the food and brought it to his mouth, sucking it. Then his teeth closed around the tip, nipping gently. "I want you."

Rose stiffened and jerked her hand away. "I don't know

anything about you, except you just may have an evil temper. Your eyes flash and I hear thunder in your voice. I'm not intimidated, of course, but nothing happens this fast. Not in Waterville, Missouri, U.S.A. Life sort of meanders into the right course, without pushing it before its time. You're a person who likes to arrange things on your schedule.''

''Why are you here?'' he asked abruptly, dismissing pleasantries. He rubbed his free hand across his bare chest and noted Rose's blue eyes following the movement. She was aware of him as a man, he decided, and yet she complicated the attraction between them. Women could be confusing. ''You aren't here to return the basket. You could have sent that with my mother or Estelle later on.''

''I didn't want the food to go to waste.''

Her answer was too petulant, too quick, and Stefan circled it. She was too wary of him and yet he admired her bravery for confronting her fears—for wanting to face down and file away any question she might have about an attraction to him. ''Yes, I am lonely,'' he said finally. ''It has been a long time since I have wanted the company of a woman. To feel a woman's skin against my own. To say these things aloud is difficult. I have had only one woman—my wife—and so it is that I am not so competent at this.''

Those blue eyes blinked and Rose looked down at the bowl she held, studying it intently. ''Don't kiss me anymore, bud,'' she whispered.

The air had stilled and warmed and trembled as Stefan studied her. ''You don't like it?''

''I think I'll be going now. Nice knowing you,'' she whispered before hurrying out the door. Stefan noted that she had not lied or attempted to disprove that she'd enjoyed that kiss on the dock and the one in her kitchen.

After her pickup skidded out of the farm's driveway, Stefan slapped his open hand against the wall. He had always considered himself to be a patient man and now he knew that with Rose, he was not.

The telephone rang; Louie had chosen the wrong moment to call. "Estelle?" he asked sharply when Stefan did not respond to his greeting.

"Louie, I think you should come here," Stefan said, after the brief pause. "There is much work to do. The chicken house needs to be cleaned and the refuse scattered on my mother's garden. You could milk the cows she is getting and help me move the outhouse. I will not offer to pay you, of course, because I know you would not accept. But you will see my daughter at odd moments—when you are not shingling the roof, or crawling beneath the house to help with the bug problem. When can we expect you?"

Louie stuttered an excuse and quickly hung up. Stefan smiled briefly. At least he had accomplished one feat—discouraging Louie from visiting Estelle. But Stefan still longed to hold Rose warm and close against him. He rubbed his bare chest, just over his heart and the ache in it. The pursuit and capture of Rose Granger would not be easy.

He heard the roaring of an engine and glanced outside to see Rose's pickup soaring into the farm driveway. It skidded to a stop and Stefan smiled. He suspected Rose's style of meeting problems was either head-on, or repeat attacks until she resolved the matter to her satisfaction. Apparently Stefan was worth a repeat attack; he took that as a good sign. He watched her hurry along the walkway and jog up the steps.

She jerked open the door, pinned him in the bald light and said, "Look. I've been attracted to guys before, okay? You're not the first."

"Okay," he answered slowly as she began to pace across the worn linoleum. Rose was struggling with her past and fear of the future. The war fascinated Stefan.

"You need new linoleum. We can make you a deal on floor coverings since you're going to need so much. Our paint sale is still on, too. This whole place could use two coats of outside paint. We give discounts when you buy twenty gallons or more at the same time. This old place will soak up the first coat. You'll need plenty of caulking, too."

"Yes, of course. Thank you for the suggestion." Stefan tried not to smile. He enjoyed watching her, this tall, lithe woman whose loyalty to her father and friends ran deep.

She placed her hands on her hips and studied him. "If you haven't been with a woman in a long time, how can you kiss like that?"

Stefan pushed away from the wall and moved toward her. He placed his hands on either side of the kitchen counter, bracketing Rose's hips. He couldn't resist stroking that soft curve of her hips with his thumbs. She was so perfect, so feminine, a delicate flower and quite possibly a very passionate woman. If she made love with the vitality she applied to everything else, he might not recover. "Like what?"

The little quiver passing through her body pleased him. She was fearless, though, eyeing him defiantly. "You're too close and you know it. You're sucking up all my air."

"You can suck up mine," he returned, enjoying the warmth of her body close to his, the fragrance of her skin, her hair.

"I know a woman who would be perfect for you," Rose whispered shakily. "Sophisticated, feminine, very good conversationalist. Maggie White is not married, her children are grown and she's a marvelous cook. She's very attractive and always wears dresses—sometimes long, flowing ones—with just the right jewelry—sometimes dangling earrings, and men seem to love being with her. She's very trendy and worldly. You might want to meet her. I can fix you up…. What's so funny?''

He ran a fingertip over the freckles on her cheek. ''Do you always talk so much when you are nervous with a man?''

She shivered again, but refused to look away. ''You're standing too close and you're not wearing a shirt.''

Stefan pressed his case; Rose needed to admit to herself that she was a very sensual woman—attractive, desirable—and that she, too, was simmering. He wanted to remove himself from the ''bud'' bin, where she tossed the other males in her life. ''You have seen men without shirts before, surely.''

''I've got a hard day tomorrow. Big paint sale and sure to have plenty of customers. I'm leaving,'' she said unevenly after a long pause. She swallowed and locked her gaze with his.

Stefan sensed that she was forcing herself not to look at his body. He nodded and stepped away from her. ''As you wish.''

She did not move. ''I feel… I feel as if you could devour me.''

''I could,'' he answered curtly, truthfully. ''But I would expect you to do a certain amount of devouring on your own.''

''I'm athletic. I run every morning that I can. I play ball. Men usually think of me as a tomboy,'' she whispered, trembling now, her hands gripping the counter behind her.

''I don't. I think of you as a desirable woman.''

She took an unsteady step away from him, then another,

and at the door she turned to stare at him. "You'll get over this. Most men do. I've been referred to as 'macho-woman.' Summer will end, and you'll be gone."

When Stefan continued to look at her, she shook her head and closed the door behind her. After her headlights faded into the night, Stefan stood a long time, alone with his thoughts and his hunger for Rose.

In the morning, his mother patted his cheek. "You had a restless night. And up so early, hammering away downstairs. It has been a long time since you have wanted to be near a woman."

"We only have a short time before my stove arrives." Stefan picked up boards and hurled them out of the open back door. "She calls me 'bud.' Like I am a brother. She wants to introduce me to a woman more suitable. Am I a man, or an old cooking pot to be passed around?"

"Some old cooking pots can be quite in demand." Yvette tossed an apple to him. "I wondered when you would come to life, and it appears that now you have."

He studied the perfect apple, which reminded him of Rose's breasts and the taste he had not managed. "Stop scowling, Stefan," his mother said. "You move too fast and you frighten her. Have patience. Let the pot simmer a while. At breakfast, it was easy to see how wary she is of you. Your arm brushed hers and she jumped. A woman likes to choose her own course. Especially a woman like Rose, who has managed by herself for quite some time. Patience, Stefan."

By noon, Estelle had complained of his bad mood and had left to pick up cleaning supplies in Waterville. While Stefan cooked on the simple farm stove, he longed for his own stainless steel range with ovens and warming shelf.

Remodeling the house, making it livable, kept his body tired, but his mind still prowled through his images of Rose.

By early afternoon, his mother was cheerfully doing laundry in the new washer and dryer, which had just arrived. Stefan made his daily call to check on the restaurants and was a little disappointed that business was running smoothly without him. Yvette peered around the corner and folded a towel as she smiled at him. "So much like your father. He couldn't believe his business could do without him."

Stefan remembered all the times he'd wanted his father to be at home. "Have I missed so much of my daughter's life?"

"No, but you have missed much of your own. You are only coming awake now, with this girl, Rose. You are only now realizing how lonely you've been. This summer will be good not only for Estelle, but for you, too, I think. You have not played since you were a very small boy. Perhaps it is time."

Stefan considered the raw blisters on his hands, the ache of his muscles and the hunger of his body. "Perhaps. Do you think Estelle misses Louie?"

Yvette laughed gaily. "No. But she doesn't want you to think that you have had your way. She wishes you to know it is her choice. You cannot keep Estelle from becoming a woman. Look outside."

Stefan frowned at the teenage girls and boys who were talking with Estelle. She looked like any country girl, healthy and laughing and flirting a bit, too. Stefan's head began to hurt. Memories of his daughter circled him—first a tiny baby, then a toddler and now she was a woman. "Since she was twelve, boys seem to be all around her. I'm losing her."

His mother shrugged. "It is life. It is not something you can stop. You did the right thing to try Estelle's dream for the summer, Stefan. You always do the right thing for your family. Perhaps it is time you started thinking of doing what is best for you. You sacrificed much too early for your father's demands, and for that I am sad. I tried, but Guy feared failure so much, and he did want the best for you. He loved you."

"Yes. And you." He had often wondered how his mother could bear such a cold man, but then bits of tenderness that he had seen filtered back to him. A woman could change a man, but could a man change a woman?

Four

"**Y**ou should see what the house looks like now. I didn't know Daddy was a carpenter. We've only lived there two weeks and, already, he's got the kitchen the way he wants it, and the house is perfect. Grandma and I had the best time at a farm auction, bidding on furniture and household things. We went to the church bazaar and to yard sales for the rest. We bargained—can you imagine that? And we traded things. Just like Grandma used to do in her village. Grandma says the best things are those that have been well-loved and she's right. They're all just great—homey and worn and soft. I've got a kitten, Jenny Linn bed and a homemade quilt just like any other country girl," Estelle said as Yvette and Rose knelt, digging carefully to uproot starts from around the abandoned log cabin.

The old cabin was falling apart, the barn no more than rusted sheet metal and broken, weathered gray boards. But some long forgotten homestead woman had loved plants

and Rose enjoyed Yvette's delight when showing the rustic
cabin, overgrown with scarlet climbing roses and circled
by peonies and violets. The lavender bed had started most
of the herb gardens in and around Waterville. The overgrown azalea bushes hid rabbits, and the field of daffodils
and tiger lilies had long lost their blooms. After a hard day
at the store, Rose hoped that ''flower rustling'' in the evening with her new friends would relax her. She'd lost too
much sleep and it was Stefan Donatien's fault. *He had set
her sensors humming and she felt as taut as a bowstring.
If she were a paint can and he touched her, she'd explode.*

Yvette carefully dug the daffodil bulbs and placed them
within the dampened newspaper for the trip home. ''Stefan
appears to have a certain amount of excess energy. He
works long into the night and he is up before my chickens.''

Rose carefully slipped her trowel beneath a cluster of
lavender, gently easing the roots from their rich earth
mooring. Stefan Donatien had cost her sleep. She didn't
want the warmth his touch had brought. She didn't want
that throbbing deep inside, aroused by the memory of his
kiss. Though Yvette and Estelle were regular customers at
the paint store, he hadn't appeared; he just might have
taken her suggestion about Maggie, a woman more suitable than Rose. Exactly why would a man like Stefan Donatien take a second look at her?

Why would he move so fast and so certain?

*How could he look so warm and simmering, so intimate
as he stood near her?*

Stefan's trial separation of Estelle and Louie seemed a
good game plan for Rose to employ, too. Stefan would get
over any notions he had after a time and everything would
settle down into the comfortable zone she preferred. She
knew she couldn't afford any unexpected sexual develop-

ments, not when she was just sliding safely into midlife's home plate. She'd already paid high prices for believing in love and romance. Whatever Stefan was offering, she couldn't afford to take. She didn't trust him, rather she didn't trust her startling reaction to him—as if she wanted to grab those wide shoulders and hold tight to see where the ride would take her.

Well, she had tried that with Mike, in a desperate effort to find romance. She'd had all the heartbreak she wanted in this lifetime. She tried to change the topic from Stefan, because he occupied enough of her thoughts already and her senses started jumping just at the mention of his name. "Dad and I are going to start shingling the roof next week. He is feeling better."

Her father seemed almost boyish when he talked about Yvette; he no longer seemed to mull the past. Yvette fascinated most of the men in Waterville and the barbershop gossip had changed from crops and machines to current feminine fashions. In the grocery store, older women were humming and bright and cheerful, the result of more attentive husbands. In the post office, the scramble for new catalogs was fierce, the demand for soft flowing dresses increased. The local dry goods store started ordering more dress fabric and sewing machines were whirring. Yvette and Estelle fitted easily into the community. Stefan seemed apart and distant; his tense argument with the cook at Danny's Café about the correct cooking of pasta had started an immediate scandal. The cook went on strike during dinner hour, and as a result, Stefan was immediately banned from Danny's, which had already excluded him from the men's morning coffee group.

"My dad is grumpy," Estelle noted as Yvette was silent, her floppy straw hat hiding her expression. "It can't be Louie, because he hasn't called for some reason. It can't be business, because according to the office secretary everything is just fine. He works late every night to keep the business running smoothly, and on top of problems. I don't know what his problem is apart from that, but he's not talking. Sometimes he just sits on the front porch and stares into the night. He looks so lonesome, sitting there alone. Sometimes I think that if he didn't have us to cook for, he'd just sit there forever.''

Rose stilled; ''alone'' meant Stefan hadn't taken up with Maggie, because she never let a man be alone until he was wrung-out and used up. Rose inhaled and her hand trembled on her trowel—but then there was plenty of Stefan to use up.

''Some things are private, *ma chérie*,'' Yvette returned gently. ''I'm so happy our new friend is helping us. This flower rustling is so much fun. Your *papa* is also having fun, I think, on that old tractor, plowing that field so early this morning. And he adores that old pickup. It's really his first chance to enjoy something he should have been allowed to do as a teenager.''

Estelle stood and shaded her eyes against the mid-May sunlight, staring toward the farm road. ''What's going on?''

Rose pushed herself upright, then reached to help Yvette rise to her feet. They watched a flood of piglets tear across the field; Zeb Black, a burly farmer, hurried behind them, panting and trying to catch his breath. Rose rubbed her hands together. ''This calls for action.''

''Count me in.'' Estelle grinned. With her black, gleaming hair in a ponytail and wearing a T-shirt and shorts and joggers, she looked like any farm girl. ''Let's go!''

''Thanks, Rose,'' Zeb called as the two women ran after the five squealing piglets. ''Old Mary, the sow, broke through the fence again, and those rascals just decided to take off...chased 'em a fair piece with the pickup. Bring 'em back to me and I'll put those little rascals in it.''

Rose caught three squirming piglets, and Estelle caught one, and Zeb seemed flustered when Yvette came to the pickup, admiring his stock. He said he didn't want her to stand too close for fear some of the mud that encrusted them—and him—might soil her "pretty dress."

A long-married man, Zeb flushed when Rose stared at him, disbelieving his gallant behavior when he barely noticed his tiny, silent wife. Rose was dripping in mud and so was Estelle. He smiled feebly at them, before they ran off after the last piglet who was headed for the farm pond. Estelle was shouting, obviously enjoying herself as they trapped the piglet, who ran back and forth between them. "Gotcha!" Rose yelled and dived for the squealing animal.

Victorious at last, she hugged the squirming prize to her, tripped and fell into the pond. Sloshing in the muddy depths and trying to regain her balance wasn't easy, but she laughed, enjoying the cheers from the bank. Then something gripped the front of her sleeveless blouse and hauled her out of the muddy water. "I got him," she exclaimed happily, hugging her squirming piglet until Zeb took him.

"Yes, you did," Stefan said, his deep voice threaded with humor.

Riding high on her victory, Rose grinned up at him. He grinned back, looking not as foreign and stern, but with a stubble covering his jaw and wearing a dirty, grease-stained T-shirt, he looked like any farmhand, just in from spring baling. He smelled like freshly cut alfalfa, a scent that she'd always enjoyed. "This is farm life, bud. I was the best greased pig catcher at the fair in my time."

"I can see that—" Stefan tensed as Rose threw her arms

around him and kissed him just as she would any good "bud."

This "bud" wrapped his arms around her quickly, tugged her close and changed the kiss into a sensuous, stormy heat. She dived into the enticing, mysterious taste and the feel of his body close to hers, and tossed away everything but the sense that the inevitable had come calling. His hands trembled on her as he lifted her off her feet and continued kissing her, his mouth slanted, fused to hers as lightning danced around them and thunder roared and her senses began an unfamiliar beat.

His lips lifted slowly from hers and she shocked herself by taking one last quick kiss, then met that dark, intense gaze with her own. "I can't breathe," she whispered.

"I'm holding you too tight?" he whispered back unevenly, his accent more pronounced.

"Not that. You're just sucking up all my air again. And you've got a definite problem," she whispered shakily. Stefan's hard thighs were pressed against her damp ones, his body taut and humming as he held her.

"You think I am happy about this?" he asked harshly. "That I act like a boy around you? That thoughts of you keep me awake?"

Somewhere in the distance, Zeb cleared his throat. "I'll just be getting these little ones back to their mama."

Stefan placed Rose back on her feet and his hot, intimate look raked down her muddy body, where her wet blouse clung to her breasts and her nipples peaked. His swallow was rough as he smoothed her damp hair from her face. "Rose," he whispered so softly, wrapping her name in the taste of midnight rendezvous, sensual touches and heart-stopping intimacy.

When Rose pulled herself out of the daze she had just slid into, she looked to find Estelle and Yvette. She hoped to use them to put distance between Stefan and herself, but they were walking across the field toward the plant starts. Clearly Stefan's family had left her to fend for herself.

"What are you doing here?" she asked him.

He motioned to his pickup on the farm road. "I needed a part for the tractor and was going into town. I could not resist stopping when I saw you and Estelle acting like happy children in the field, chasing those pigs. Estelle has never looked so young and free. It was a beautiful thing to see, and to hear your laughter. You've become friends with my mother and my daughter. It seems that is more than I can do."

"We were flower rustling," Rose explained shakily, as Stefan carefully took a clean white handkerchief and began methodically wiping her face, holding it gently with one hand. She heard herself talking and knew it was because she was so nervous, her skin heating as he touched her. "It's an old custom here for new homemakers in Waterville to take a piece of this beautiful old home-place to theirs...an inheritance, so to speak. Taking those starts thins out the bulbs and lets the plants grow better. Sometimes people come out here to separate the plants and start them at another place on the farm, like those willows over there. It's a family sort of thing to do. You know, like Grandma Granger did when she was a girl, and like Mom and Dad did when they were dating, and like— Lily of the Valleys are pretty down in that hollow...little white bells on dark broad leaves—"

"Why did you kiss me?" Stefan asked softly. His intimate study of her face, her eyes, her cheeks and mouth took away her breath.

"You were there," she answered truthfully. "It seemed right after catching the pig. I had to celebrate somehow."

"I would like to carry you off and feast upon you," Stefan said raggedly. "Do you not know how seductive you are—part girl, so innocent, and all woman?"

"'Seductive?'" Rose circled the thought. "You're mistaken. Not one of my—"

"They were blind fools," Stefan said passionately. "I do not want to hear about them."

His command shifted Rose's unsteady emotions into simmering anger. In her lifetime, no one had spoken sharply to her, or ordered her. "Oh, you don't? And I don't like your tone. Take it back."

Stefan blinked as if she had reached out and struck him. "Take what back?"

"That high-handed order, like you were a general or something."

He was silent for a moment, his expression darkening. "Perhaps I speak too formally to you. I was born in this country, but sometimes my upbringing—some schooling in France—emerges when I am…emotional. My father spoke thus—very proper—when he was…emotional."

Stefan shook his head as if a new thought had entered it and he wasn't certain of it or himself. He started again. "You arouse me. I do not like that I am so susceptible to your touch, but I am. You think I like to think of you with other men?"

Rose held up her hands. Stefan was volatile and cruising off into areas of her life that even she didn't want to examine too closely. "Let's get back on course. There's nothing between us. There isn't going to be."

"Is that so?" Then Stefan reached out one hand, curled it around the back of her neck and tugged her close. She pushed at his chest and then, failing to dislodge herself, stood staring defiantly up at him. "So you decide what is to be, do you not? You open yourself to no one, especially me. I am too old, you think? I am not suitable? You wound me, *ma chérie*,'' he said in a scathing tone, his accent more pronounced.

''Do you have to be so darned open about what you're thinking?'' she demanded and realized that Stefan's other hand had settled firmly on her bottom, caressing it, as if her curves pleased him. Stefan was the first man to look at her like that, to touch her as if he had all the time in the world to enjoy her. She began to shiver, her nerves dancing as if they needed to lock on to an anchor—

Suddenly Stefan bent, picked her up on his shoulder and carried her to the pond. When he tossed her into the water, it was cold, and mud sucked at her feet as she struggled free. Rose didn't think; anger pushed her out of the pond. She ran at Stefan, who was walking back to his pickup, and hit him with a linebacker's tackle.

He went down in the field grass, turned, grabbed her and pinned her beneath him. Rose frowned up at him, her wrists clasped by his hands. Stefan's grin flashed; he lowered his head and took her mouth in a devastating kiss. It was a rough, hungry kiss, and not the kind that she could stop—if she'd wanted to, if she weren't grabbing him with her arms and legs and wrestling him beneath her to have more of that fiery, wide-open hunger. She raised up once to look at him, to stop the whirling furnace, and Stefan stared back at her, his dark expression just as wild and fierce as she felt. Then he looked down at her breasts, to the buttons that had opened to reveal her lacy bra. His body hardened beneath hers, and in the next second that dark, heated gaze was slowly easing away from her face, from her lips, and rising to Yvette and Estelle who were standing near them. Yvette was trying to hide a grin and Estelle was staring down at them, her expression shocked.

Her mouth moved once and no sound came, and then, *"Daddy! Just what are you doing?"*

"Playing. Rose likes to play. I think she wants me," he said unevenly, though his expression would have been sheepish, if he weren't Stefan Donatien, power business-man. "Go away."

"Stay," Rose ordered and couldn't seem to push herself upright, away from Stefan's big, aroused body…or the se-ductive stroking of his hands on her back. She blinked when she saw her fingers pressed deep into his strong shoulders.

"That's the first time Daddy has ever—" Estelle mur-mured in a disbelieving tone.

"I know, dear," Yvette said cheerfully. She tugged on Estelle's arm and began walking toward the old cabin. "Let's go take my new plants home. It will be a nice little walk. Coming, Rose? Stefan?"

"Not me," Rose stated firmly as she eased herself to her feet. She was headed for safety—anywhere away from Stefan. "I'm going home."

Standing beside her now, Stefan lightly tugged her wet hair and Rose swatted at him. Estelle and Yvette were having an animated conversation as they walked, which became more energetic each time Estelle looked back at her father. With as much dignity as Rose could manage, she marched off across the field toward town, her shoes filled and squishing with mud.

She couldn't resist turning, just that once, to see Stefan standing in the lush green field, his arms crossed over his chest. His boyish, devastating grin shot straight across the dying sunlight and hit her with the force of a thunderbolt. She turned to stare at him and his expression changed into a darker, sensual one that caused every molecule in her body to vibrate and heat.

She couldn't—Rose swallowed the tight emotion in her throat. She'd been through enough pain and she couldn't expose herself again. She forced herself to turn and walk away, and then she began to run. She ran until she thought her heart would burst—just like it did when her mother left her.

At her house, a cold shower did not erase Stefan's arousing touch, the intimate way he looked at her. Rose shook her head beneath the spray. "I can't help it if I'm a physical woman. I feel like all my senses have been sleeping, just waiting to leap on Stefan. I didn't feel like this with Larry or Henry or Mike, no matter how much I tried. This is just *not* fair. I've just now got my life under control. *I was safe.* I will not get involved with Stefan. He'll get tired of dull rural life in Waterville and he'll move on. And he's just too—just too unsafe," she finished saying.

She blew the water from her bottom lip, the lip that Stefan had gently suckled. Still sensitive and tasting him, Rose Granger decided that in the ball game of life, she wasn't meant to have fair and just umpire calls. Dressed in a long emerald caftan, with her damp hair propped high on her head, she went out on the porch to curl up in the white wicker chair, to sip lemonade and to contemplate while she painted her toenails. She always fought life better with scarlet toe nails and with Stefan, she was certain there would be a battle.

In the evening hours, Henry and Shirley strolled by. They stopped at Rose's front white picket fence. "Heard you were rolling in the mud with Stefan Donatien," Henry called. "Heard you pinned him in five seconds flat."

"Hi, Shirley. Keep on moving, Henry. No offense," Rose answered and frowned as they moved off and Henry's guffaws carried back on the sweet May air.

From the other side of the hedge that Mrs. Wilkins was shearing, she called merrily, "I heard that, too, Rose. Zeb was thankful you're such a good pig catcher, though."

"Next time he can catch them himself," Rose muttered.

"What was that you said? Yes, that Donatien man would be a good catch," Mrs. Wilkins agreed. "But he's not apt to let you roam free like those other boys. He's the man-kind that would want a ring on your finger to brand you as his. He's the real up-close-and-personal type."

"I'm going in the house, Mrs. Wilkins. Have a nice night." Rose closed her eyes and tried not to think of Stefan, which was difficult since he was opening her front picket gate and walking through it. He had showered, shaved and she resented how delicious he looked—coming up the steps with that wildflower bouquet in one hand and a picnic basket in the other.

"No more picnics with you," she said bluntly and wished she were wearing underwear. When she shifted restlessly, Stefan's dark eyes immediately locked on to her breasts; he had that hot, steaming look that both terrified and excited her. The evening air carried the scent of the flowers, the good food and Stefan, a heady combination. "I'm all done with erotic stuff and I'm on a diet," she added, so that he wouldn't mistake the way she couldn't breathe or take her eyes off him.

"Tell me about your mother, Rose," Stefan said quietly as he began to unpack the picnic basket, in quick efficient motions.

"You do that like you were a waiter," she said, as he whipped out a linen tablecloth and smoothed it over the small, round table between the wicker chairs. She didn't want to reveal her deeply hoarded feelings about her mother, the terrible pain of abandonment, the decline of her father. She suspected that Stefan was very thorough and she didn't want him prowling so close to pain she'd stuffed away for years.

In a short time, she'd learned that Stefan was very likely to be efficient at everything he did—including kissing. She didn't want to think about his lovemaking techniques.

"I started waiting tables when I was very young. Before that, my father would tutor me as to the right wines, the right glasses, the right breads, cheeses and sauces. Your mother?" he repeated, as he poured red wine into a glass and handed it to her. He settled into the other wicker chair and spread paté on crackers, artistically arranging them on the plate before taking his own wineglass.

"Your wife?" she countered, reaching for her second cracker and paté. She didn't want him to know about the dark corners of her life; he knew enough already.

"I loved her. Not a passionate love, but it was warm and soft and good. It was more than I had hoped for in a girl matching my background—"

"Matching your money?" she asked, anxious to point out the differences between them.

"Our families knew each other," he returned quietly with a nod.

"An arranged marriage?"

Stefan looked out into the evening, as though settling into the past. "It happens, and I did love her. When she gave me Estelle, I thought we were complete. But Claire's heart was delicate, and childbirth weakened her. Estelle was only ten when her mother gave up the struggle. I will always regret the time I spent away from them both, building the restaurant business. For a long time, Estelle blamed herself for her mother's death—she may still—and I didn't suspect until much later…I was too busy, you see."

Rose knew exactly how a child could blame herself for

circumstances she couldn't control. On the porch, Stefan's shadows surrounded him and Rose didn't think—she acted. She patted his jeaned knee and asked, "Hey, bud. Are these crackers all there is to eat?"

Stefan smiled gently. "You always give to others, don't you? Trying to help them? You have a soft heart, *ma chérie*."

"I'm just hungry, bud. Don't read more into it than that," she lied lightly and tried to let the shadows hide her blush. Stefan looked as if he needed a friend—or a lover. She didn't want to be his lover, but she knew how to be a good friend. "You know what this looks like, don't you? People are already gossiping about us. I don't want to get them all stirred up and expecting more than they're going to get."

"Well, getting stirred up can be quite—exciting," Stefan murmured, humor threaded through his deep voice. "When you are ready, I would like you to tell me about your mother, but for now, let us eat."

Rose wished she could have refused his meal, but her stomach clenched at the sight of the light dinner, a lovely dome of spaghetti noodles, artichokes, eggs and cooked ham. "Yum," she said, before diving into the plate Stefan handed to her.

He ate more slowly, serving her a second helping. "You eat without stopping. Do you ever relax fully without charging into your next project?"

"This is good, but I would really like to top it off with a hot dog and plenty of mustard," she managed to say around the salad she was eating. She stared meaningfully at Larry and Mary Lou who were trying not to be too obvious. They slowly cruised by her house, taking stealthy looks.

Stefan breathed deeply, but did not respond to her hot

dog comment. Instead he began methodically, grimly packing the food and plates back into his basket. "I can see your breasts through that material," he said finally, pinning her with his dark, intimate look. "And I want you. But I want to be your friend, too. You give, but you do not accept the same in return. Your defenses are high, Rose Granger. You fear a broken heart and you trust little. This makes the journey to your heart and hopefully to your bed, a difficult one."

"Do you always have to come straight to the point?" she asked, crossing her arms in front of her. Stefan could jar every cell in her body with that look. Now, standing and leaning against the front porch post, his cotton shirt unbuttoned above his crossed arms and wearing jeans like any other Waterville male, Stefan took her breath away.

She could have leaped upon him and dragged him up to her bed. Rose forced herself back to the garden of reason, picking out the weeds of temptation. She'd only known him for over two weeks; he came from a different world. He would be leaving, once boredom hit him—or the summer ended—and she'd be left in a dark, depressing hole.

"Yes, I do always come to the point," he said unevenly. As he spoke quietly, he smiled at Mrs. Wilkins, who was peering over the hedge.

"You know," Mrs. Wilkins said, "the last time Rose had man-trouble, she painted that whole big two-story house by herself, then redid every room in it. In the summer, I had my windows open and I could hear her crying over that no-good who dumped her. I'm getting old and I'm not in the mood to hear that poor girl cry again. You'd just better have good intentions."

"Mrs. Wilkins, thank you—but I can handle this," Rose

said, loving the woman who had tried to ease her mother's desertion. "I'm thirty-seven now, you know."

"I changed your diapers, Miss Sass. Don't think the whole town isn't buzzing about this man paying so much attention to you."

"I assure you, Mrs. Wilkins, my intentions are purely—" Stefan shot Rose a sultry look, then murmured, "honorable."

"Here in Waterville, people take their time courting and when they do, there's usually a wedding ring at the end of it," Mrs. Wilkins persisted staunchly, unswayed by Stefan's deep, seductive voice. "Rose ought to have a flock of children around her by now, but since she doesn't, I'd guess you'd better leave well enough alone. She's pretty well over the hill for that game."

"Thank you, Mrs. Wilkins. I think you've pretty well said all there is to be said." Rose's life had always been an open book to the people of Waterville. When she was growing up, most of them had either fed her or patched her scraped knees. As they aged, she'd started taking care of some of them—not because she felt an obligation, but because she loved them. Their lives fitted together like one of the old pioneer quilts, worn and soft and comfortable. She knew they meant well, and she tried not to show her heartbreak because they worried for her.

She stared meaningfully at Stefan. Stefan looked more like lover material, than like that of a husband. Rose didn't want to dip into dreams safely tucked away. Just looking at him caused her body to hum and she didn't want to get started all over again—she suspected that Stefan could leave even more scars than Mike. "One of you has to leave. I'd prefer it was you."

"Very well. But I want you to think about this—we started off wrong, but I have waited too long for a woman like you. According to what your father told my mother, you fixed up Henry with Shirley and Larry with Mary Lou. Maggie White has started hunting me and I want you to call her off. I cannot oblige Maggie's not-so subtle invitation to her bed, because I intend to be in yours.''

With that, he lifted her palm up to his lips and pressed a kiss into the center.

''You know how you are, dear,'' Mrs. Wilkins called while Rose tried to slow her heart. ''Too sweet and soft and naive for big-city men. Better shoo him away before you get all tangled up again.''

Stefan's sultry look took in Rose's blush. ''Yes,'' he said very quietly. ''I would like to be tangled up with you.''

The first of June marked the Donatiens' one-month anniversary on their Waterville farm. For Stefan, it marked two long weeks without that enjoyable sparring with Rose. He sat on the porch he had just repaired, tipped back his chair against the side of the house, propped his bare feet up on the railing and gave himself to the sweet early-summer night.

A reasonable man, he told himself as he ran his hand across his chest, would give a woman time. When his daughter spoke of her friend, Rose, his heart shouldn't stop, his mind sliding back to how she looked, dressed in that emerald lounging gown and curled upon the wicker chair. He'd been too blatant, telling her of his need for her. With the fireflies blinking in the June night, the scent of his mother's garden wrapped around him, Stefan tried not to think of Rose. He tried not to think of how she looked when he'd come into town that early morning. She'd been jogging, her damp T-shirt plastered to her breasts, which bobbed gently. Her shorts had fluttered around her smooth bottom, those long legs eating up the road.

He'd give her time to think, Stefan promised himself as the vision of Rose, all hot and sweaty and sexy raced through his mind. Then he stopped thinking and breathing as Rose's pickup pulled in front of the house. Dressed in her usual T-shirt and cutoff shorts, Rose stalked up the walkway, her thongs slapping against her soles. "I want to talk with you," she said bluntly, tapping her hand against her bare thigh. "I see no point in beating around the bush, while you're the cause of all my problems. So I've come right to grab the bull by the horns as we say hereabouts."

She blinked, hesitated as though she were replaying her own words and pushed on. "I wanted to talk with you privately...Estelle is at my house watching a video with her friends. I know your mother is with my dad—and I'm not certain I like how he's acting lately, all sappy and happy—enough to make Maggie White take notice. She called to see what was making him seem so frisky. He bought new aftershave and new undershorts, all by himself, a sure sign that he's up to something."

Stefan removed his feet from the railing and stood abruptly. "We have a television. Why is Estelle not here, in my house? She refuses to bring her friends—"

Rose stared off into the night. "Would you put on a shirt? Just as mosquito protection?" she added, and in the slight glow of the citronella candle, her face seemed rosy.

Five

Maybe this wasn't such a good idea, Rose thought as she tried to avoid looking at Stefan. He stood on his front porch, watching her approach on the stone walkway to the Donatien farmhouse. She picked her way through the scent of the insect-repelling citronella candle to the one of a freshly showered man. Stefan's chest gleamed in the candlelight, that wedge of dark hair still beaded with water. His jeans were opened at the top snap and the worn places in them evidenced the all-male package beneath. She tried to swallow and failed, because she'd never seen a man's feet look so—big and bold and strong. When he locked them in that wide-legged stance, he looked as if nothing could move him. He looked as dependable as a mountain, as hot as July and as tasty as Mrs. Wilkins's strawberry jam on buttered, freshly baked bread. Rose fought the ripple of desire within her and damned it for taking a sweeter course.

Stefan's black hair was still damp and curling. Rose thought of how a sweet little baby would look with those curls—the idea caused her hands to grip the railing as an anchor...because her knees were giving way at the thought. Long ago, she'd forced the door closed on dreams of her own children and settled into the safe lane of god-mothering.

Pain shot through her and she regretted the soft cry that escaped her keeping. Instantly Stefan reached for her hands, turning them upward for his inspection. The raw blisters left by removing shingling nails mocked her. Stefan's grim silence demanded an explanation. "I've been shingling," she said. "I had to put it off because business was so good at the store and I pulled off a good quarter of the roof today. I didn't want Dad up on our two-story roof and I was really feeling up to tearing something apart."

"You will wait here while I get the antibacterial cream and gauze to wrap your hands," Stefan ordered as he placed his hand on her shoulder and firmly pushed her down onto a chair. In a heartbeat, the front storm door closed behind him.

Rose sat in the quiet night, the fireflies blinking in their mating patterns, and wondered how Stefan could take the breath right from her with one look.

"I should be going," she whispered as he came back to the porch, kneeled at her side and began intently applying the cream. She felt a little light-headed with all the intoxicating scents of man and soap and Stefan and summer night curling around her.

Stefan closed the tube, placed it aside and gently wrapped the gauze around her hands. Then, in one swift motion, he scooped her up. Still holding her, he eased into the big old rocking chair.

"Now, this is silly," she whispered, trying to sit upright and away from all that darkly tanned chest, and the enticing wedge of hair. He'd shocked her, treating her as if she weren't a tomboy and muscle-packed and independent and unavailable.

Stefan eased her head upon his shoulder and began rocking her slowly.

"I want to cry, and I don't know why," she whispered as her throat thickened with emotions she didn't understand. Stefan's lips brushed lightly across her forehead, her brows, her lashes. His kisses weren't helping her unstable condition. She thought that she could stay here forever, with his big, safe body beneath her, his skin against her cheek. His thumb caressed her wrist, just there, where she was too vulnerable. He made her feel unique, delicate and feminine. Unable to resist, she rubbed her cheek against him.

Stefan stilled, then his hand cupped her chin, lifting her face to his. "How have I caused you trouble?" he asked gently.

Looking up into that rugged face and dark, seductive gaze, Rose tried to focus. "I can't think just now. Things are just too complicated. Give me a minute."

"Okay." Stefan smiled tenderly, then brushed his lips against hers. Lightning went zigzagging through her veins, struck her heart and made it race. Thunder rumbled in her blood and her skin suddenly felt too tight.

"You didn't make a bet, did you?" she heard herself ask. Her heart would never recover if Stefan had acted like Mike.

He frowned slightly. "Bet?"

"That you could get to me."

The seductive smile returned and Stefan kissed her again, lightly and gently, as if he were seeking something

precious from her. "I didn't make a bet, but am I getting
to you?"

"I'd be foolish—with my background in men—to give
in to this." Rose trembled as Stefan's sizzling-hot look
swept over her face and her body.

He urged her hips toward him, his hand smoothing her
bottom and up her back, across her shoulders. Everything
inside Rose seemed to clench, despite her restraining order
on her body. He looked down to where her breasts nestled
against his bare chest, closed his eyes and groaned shakily.
He leaned his head back against the rocker and through
his lashes, studied her. "Why have you come?" he asked
huskily.

Sitting on a man's lap—which she hadn't done in her
lifetime, with the exception of her father—gave a woman
certain rights, Rose decided. She lifted her wrapped hand
and extended a fingertip to smooth the line between his
brows. "For Estelle. And for you," she added, letting that
fingertip roam across his thick, fascinating brows. Stefan
was a man of textures, of passion and of control. She wondered just how controlled; what she could do to tempt
him— He held very still beneath her touch, but the jerk
of muscle beneath his jaw said he wasn't exactly calm.
Rose smoothed that taut muscle, wanting to ease his trouble. That was what she did best—understand pain.
"You're too controlled for your own good, Stefan. You've
got to lighten up. Estelle has some idea that you're keeping
Louie away from her on purpose, which you have admitted
to me. She's invited him to come, but Louie always has
an excuse. And you glare at the boys in her new crowd,
especially when one of them gets too close."

"They are too easy and too quick to touch her, to put
their arms around her," Stefan stated roughly.

"You're touching me," Rose reminded him as she

looked pointedly to where his hand was stroking her thigh. Rose decided to put that action into the erotic bin, especially the movement of his thumb, just there on the inside of her thigh.

"Do not be foolish. You are a woman. I am a man. I care for you. You entice me. Fascinate me. Excite me. I am not a man who relates easily to anyone, but in you, I find...contentment."

Rose tried to recover from his rapid statements, her emotions buffeting her. She smoothed his jaw again and realized that he had eased his taut defense slightly. She ran her fingertips across those blunt, wide cheekbones and had the sense she was easing all the brooding storms within him. "You're a good father, Stefan. Estelle will make the right choices. You have to give her a chance to explore them first, though. You've got to stop being so bossy. And never, ever say 'I forbid you.'"

He exhaled as though he had been holding his breath. "In this case, I know what is best for my daughter. Louie undoubtedly has fast-moving sperm. She will not have a chance to know herself until years have passed. He will keep her pregnant and waiting on him to insure his grasp on what our family has worked so hard to keep. I would love grandchildren, but without Louie's inherited fish-mouth. Yes, it's true. He has a mouth like a fish and a mind that serves his own purposes. He would not, for one moment, consider my daughter's welfare or happiness. I caught him in my office copy room with one of the temporary help. They were not studying the menus. I could not bring myself to tell Estelle. And I could not hit him, as much as I wanted to—he is small and slight and wears dark glasses all the time."

Rose studied him, seeing all the stormy passages inside and knowing without explanation that Stefan wanted the best for his family. "It's been hard on you, hasn't it? Trying to take your father's place in business and then playing the role of both parents for Estelle?"

"You feel so much. You know so much." He kissed the gauze covering her palm and held it gently to his cheek. "I wasn't a good parent to Estelle." The admission came raggedly, as though it was the first time he had dragged it into the air. "I worked long hours. Too long and suddenly she wasn't a baby anymore. I didn't even spend the time with Claire that I should have—and she was so fragile. It was as if Estelle was a baby, and then suddenly she is a woman, and I don't understand anything—except that I am making the same mistakes as my father made with me. I am too harsh with her. I am used to managing business, not a family. The ease between your father and you does not flow between Estelle and myself. In business, I am not...sweet. I come home tired and too quick to snap at her about Louie, or her hair or that blue nail polish she used to wear. I work for hours after dinner. It's different here. It's good. She is very happy here. She has a glow about her. I never realized how much she really wanted this life. I was too involved with business. Perhaps here, she can find some small bit of what she's wanted."

Stefan frowned and held her slightly away. "Why am I causing you trouble?" he asked again.

"Everyone is talking about how you kissed me...that unbrotherly way, and then how you dropped me. They're feeling sorry for me again and I don't like it. You're not staying here any longer than it takes and I'll be left to deal with the pitiful looks of people I've known all my life. The tuna casseroles will start to arrive with the poor-old-maid looks, and then people will invite me to visit for Sunday dinner to meet their unmarried cousin, what's-his-name. He'll either be a total zero, or he'll have a houseful of children who won't want a stepmother.''

''What about your own children?'' Stefan asked softly as he studied his fingertip, which had just come to gently circle Rose's breast. Her nipple peaked beneath her T-shirt and bra. She shivered and stared at him, trying to fight the raging storm within her. Stefan stared back, and the inches between their faces seemed charged with electricity looking for a place to zap. She couldn't move as his hand slowly enclosed her breast, so gently, as if it were petals. She tried to breathe, to focus, as he caressed her and slowly moved his hand lower to find the hem of her T-shirt.

Rose hadn't been touched so carefully, so lightly and gently, and Stefan's dark gaze burned at her as though he were waiting for her reaction, and giving her a choice to reject or welcome him. By the time his hand slid upward, she was certain her heart would race away from her keeping into the night. Stefan bent his head to kiss her throat, behind her ear, her cheek, and the warm beat of his heart seemed to wait for her answer. She feared answering the needs of her body, to take the invitation of the hardened body beneath her. ''My batting average isn't good in this department,'' she managed to say finally. ''I have three ex-fiancés.''

''You seem to do exceedingly well, *ma chérie*,'' Stefan murmured as he nuzzled her throat and trailed kisses to her breast. Once there, he gently suckled in a rhythm that caused Rose to cry out and to lock her arms around him, holding him close.

Just there, on the edge, with Stefan's breath uneven against her skin, the night soft and sweet around her, she sensed him withdrawing and rearranging her clothing. When she finally opened her eyes, it was to the blinding light of head beams and the reality that Stefan was thoroughly aroused beneath her. His hands pressed her close against him and a telling shudder racked his big body. "It appears that privacy is a problem," he stated grimly as two women moved up the walkway to the house. "Hello, Mother. Hello, Estelle."

"I was just leaving," Rose said as she pushed free of Stefan, stood shakily and hurried past his mother and daughter. "Good night."

She hadn't intended to nick the Donatien's gate with her pickup's fender. The post had seemed to leap out at her while she was thinking of Stefan holding her, that big body taut against her and the pulsing, wild rhythm surging between them. *"I cannot go through this again,"* she muttered.

Stefan crouched on Rose's roof, studying the delicate bare feet, which were resting on her windowsill, the lace curtain fluttering over her ankles. At five-thirty in the morning, Waterville was quiet, dawn pushing away the night—a restless night for Stefan, with desire pounding at him, his body awakening after years. Rose's soft cries of pleasure had curled through his night, the taste of her body feeding his desire.

He had already been working for an hour, tearing off the old shingles and removing the nails. Rose's abused hands were a reflection of her emotions, of her fear of loving and being deserted. Stefan scowled at those slender, curved feet, fighting the anger within him. *To think that a man would make bets on such a loving woman, who cared for all those around her.*

The lace curtains fluttered delicately around her ankles and Stefan couldn't resist stroking the vulnerable curve of her insole. Her toes wiggled and he smiled at the red polish, a contrast to the natural woman.

Suddenly the curtains were ripped aside. Rose stared blankly at him, shrieked and grabbed the curtains. A clump sounded behind them as the curtain rod tore free and slanted out of the window. Worried for Rose, Stefan grimly wrapped the yards of white froth in his fists and pushed it through the window. He glimpsed Rose, struggling to her feet, her rocking chair upended on the floor. She grabbed the lace, hurled it aside and peered through the open window at Stefan. *"What are you doing here?"*

If he hadn't been staring at her breasts through the thin material of her shortie nightgown, he might have been able to speak. "Never have I wanted to tear a woman's clothing away," he heard himself whisper raggedly. "But I want to see all of you."

She grabbed the lace curtain and held it up to her, a blush warming her cheeks. She blinked rapidly and said, "You're wearing a tool belt and knee pads and *you're on my roof.*"

"I'm finishing the roofing. You are not to come out here."

"Stefan, people will talk. They know that I do most of the home repairs. They're still talking about my attempt at plumbing. 'Rose's great plumbing episode,' that's what they call it."

"Well, then. They'll know that I haven't dropped you as you said last night. They'll know that the romance continues with Rose Granger. Did you sleep well last night?" he asked and heard his own uncertainty.

"My feet got too hot—that's all. I stick them out the window sometimes. I like the drift of the lace across my skin. Last night—you kissing me—had nothing to do with my...um, inability to sleep," she added firmly.

Stefan studied her flushed face and couldn't resist the laughter and happiness bubbling within him. "You're fibbing, Rose. You are a very sensual woman. You kissed me back. Would you like me to come in there and prove it?''

He was enjoying her sweet, wide-eyed look when a boy called up to him, ''Hey, Mr. Donatien. You want me to put you on my paper route? After I finish my bike route, my dad takes me out in the country.''

Stefan glanced down at the boy, and at Mrs. Wilkins, and at several other townspeople, including Rose's two ex-fiancés who were scowling up at him. Those dressed in jogging gear had apparently spread the word that he was on Rose's roof. On their way to work, others had pulled their vehicles against the curb. The early morning fishermen sat in their lawn chairs on the back of pickups, sipping coffee. Rose was beloved by Waterville's residents, and her roof visitor was clearly under suspicion and surveillance by the curious crowd. ''Get in here,'' she said grimly behind him, and tugged on his T-shirt.

''She needs her roof reshingled,'' he called to the small crowd below. He couldn't resist, ''She needs me—''

''*Get in here,*'' Rose ordered more firmly and with both hands pulled his shirt. Stefan had the heady notion that she was claiming him for her own, protecting him. He eased his tall body through her open window and hung the curtain rod that Rose pushed into his hands. He'd never felt so good, so free and happy and couldn't help his grin as Rose frowned at him, pushing her hair back from her face. She jammed a tattered old flannel robe over her short nightgown and glared at him. Her father's snore sounded through the rose-spattered wallpaper. Stefan watched, fascinated by Rose's stormy, frustrated expression, as she stalked the length of the room, her long legs flashing beneath the folds of the robe. He righted the small rocking chair, perfect for a woman, and studied her feminine bedroom—the mussed bed, the pillows on the floor, the family pictures on the wall and the cotton summer dress hanging on the closet door.

"Well, what's next?" she demanded. "You can't go out the window—"

"Breakfast is next," Stefan answered, before drawing her into his arms. This time she came more easily, he noted, all fresh and warm and fragrant from sleep. Her lips gave him more than he'd ever known, her arms locked tightly around his neck, her body arching to his. He caught her closer, wanting more of her, of that natural sweetness that was Rose's alone. When her fingers caught his hair, her lips parting beneath his, Stefan fought his need to lay her on the bed, and eased her away. "Breakfast in twenty minutes," he whispered against her lips. "Then I'm finishing the roof."

There were other things he wanted to finish, Stefan thought grimly as he whipped eggs for an omelet. The image of Rose in her little nightie caught him and he swallowed—very little kept him from going upstairs to... It was a good thing his mother sent a good supply, he decided, as he opened the back door and called to the small crowd staring up at Rose's window— "Breakfast!"

Late that night, in the bedroom that served as his office, Stefan replaced the business telephone he used to communicate with his main office. He sat back from his desk, rubbed his hands over his face and groaned when his aching muscles protested. The price for showing off for Rose had settled into his body and he resented the long night without her in his bed. He turned to his mother and daughter who had just entered the room, their expressions a mix of humor and love. "Rose called you, no doubt. I cooked breakfast for half the town this morning and then her two ex-fiancés helped me finish the roof, so that I could be gone from her. They suspect I will hurt her, you see. In the middle of the pregnant one's logical argument about why I should leave Rose alone, she came up to the roof and started some nonsense about reclaiming her life and territory. She waves her hands when she is emotional. The one who admits to sharing his pregnant wife's symptoms had to lie on the roof for a time because of his morning sickness. Rose went immediately to his side, cradling his head and stroking his brow. The sheriff's loudspeaker asked if Rose needed help, and if the pregnant one was lying so still because I'd hit him. Then the sheriff came up to help finish the Grangers' roof. There is no privacy in this entire town...and I am sore from muscles I have not used. It does not help to know that I am old and out of shape.''

Yvette shook her head. ''Poor Stefan. Brooding about how he is to come back into life.''

''Daddy, you can't just take control of her. You act as if she were a business you were planning to take over— or a kitchen that you needed rearranged. Rose has managed her life and her father's for the most part. She's run her own business, and she's had terrible heartbreak. She's very independent and you're pushing too hard.''

Stefan bit into the apple that Yvette had just handed him with a plate of cheese and crusty bread. He studied the apple and placed it aside as he remembered the shape of Rose's two perfect breasts. ''Women,'' he finally muttered as his daughter came to kiss his cheek and his mother kissed the other side.

''It's because you are so protective, Stefan,'' Yvette stated gently. ''You feared that something would happen if you did not control everything, make us safe. When your father suddenly died of a heart attack, you tried so hard. Rose is not a woman to have her life controlled.''

''I am frustrated,'' Stefan admitted unevenly. He was unused to spreading his needs before his family; for years he had tried not to worry them. ''I want the best for her. She is angry at me.''

''Poor Daddy,'' Estelle murmured with humor.

''You think this is funny,'' he said, studying her. *When had she become so lovely, so caring? How much of her life had he missed?*

''Very.'' This time, she was grinning at him. ''Daddy, if you're worried about that one gray hair, there are dyes for men now, though I can't see you using them...so far as I know, you have never dated, even when women pursued you. I bet you don't know how.''

The truth, spoken by his daughter, nettled Stefan. ''Of course, I do. What could there be to dating? Dinner, dancing and—''

Estelle crossed her arms and shook her head. ''Not very inventive.''

A mouthwatering vision of how he'd want a date with Rose to end, danced through his head. Stefan wondered what to do with this girl, his daughter—the woman. On impulse, he reached for her and tickled her until she squealed and squirmed. ''You think you are too old for that, huh?'' he asked as she giggled.

The family telephone rang and she ran out of the room. Yvette lifted her eyebrows. ''My, my. You're changing, Stefan. Not so grim. This move—or someone—has also been good for you.''

''And you. I saw several men around you in the hardware store. You seem to enjoy country life.''

''I like men, you know that. I like the look of them, the fresh-shaved smell, the way they talk. I always have. But you know that I have never given my heart, or my body to any man but your father. By the way, do you need anything at the lumberyard? Oh, and we didn't know what had happened at Rose's until you told us. Stop pushing her so hard and let her make up her own mind and come to you.''

''It seems to be my nature to push. I have to go back to Chicago. Another restaurant is courting our chefs and business manager. Will you be all right here?''

''Stefan, I am at my happiest. I feel so good. My first batch of cheese is in the wooden rounds and aging. The mushrooms are growing in the root cellar, I'm preserving jams and the pleasure I have from feeding my chickens and gardening has added even more joy. I love milking cows, the daily routine with animals who return the love you give to them. With your father, it was necessary to live in the city, but I am most at home in the country. Will you bring Louie back with you? Or will you take Rose with you?''

''A definite no to the first part, and the second thought is a good idea.''

Estelle ran back into the room, her face alight. ''Daddy, it's Rose on the telephone, and she's really mad. I think she wants a showdown, like in the Western movies. She wants to pay you for the roofing job and she said that check for your day's work at the store hasn't cleared her bank account. She wants to know if you want her to write another one, adding on the roofing job.''

Stefan listened to the crickets in the June night. He wanted privacy for the discussion he wanted with Rose, away from interruptions. He wanted her for himself. Rose wasn't a woman to wait, once she'd made up her mind. If his plan worked, she would come to him. ''Tell Rose that

I'm busy and I'm leaving for Chicago in the morning. I'll talk to her when I get back in a month or so.''

''It's been two weeks since I tried to talk with you and you wouldn't answer,'' Rose began as she sat facing Stefan, across his massive office desk. She was glad she had chosen the black business suit, despite the mid-June heat in Chicago. She wanted to present a picture of an independent, knowledgeable woman who knew exactly what she was doing at all times. She'd never traveled and the safety of Waterville was far away. Despite the strange hurried ways of the city, she was determined; she wanted her discussion with Stefan to be businesslike and effective.

She tried to focus on her mission. Stefan had to see how unsuitable they were for each other; she wanted to pay her roofing debt to him. She did not want to owe Stefan anything. Just moments before, she'd been stunned by the expensively groomed power-businessman who had her ushered into his meeting with associates. His answer to the competing company who wanted his chefs was to buy them out. He wasted no time in itemizing details, or arranging dismissal of the top executives who had tried to undermine Donatien's operation. With the exception of a few tender moments in which he recognized her presence, Stefan was curt and to the point. He had finalized the meeting with a cold nod.

His associates had slanted Rose curious looks, her inexpensive black suit, blue blouse and practical walking shoes at odds with the sleek interior of the office. Stefan had briefly introduced her, had given her a light kiss as though greeting an old friend and then had asked her to stay while business was concluded.

The man facing her across the desk did not look like the man who had kissed her after the piglet-episode. His

expression was grim and taut as if he'd lost too much
sleep. She ached for the shadows beneath his eyes and the
lines between his brows and bracketing his mouth.

"It's pretty dramatic, isn't it? Coming all this way to
set me straight?" Stefan stated quietly, looking too powerful in his expensive gray business suit. His whiskey-
brown eyes drifted warmly over her and his grim expression seemed to ease. "Come here."

The anger that had simmered since the night she'd tried
to set the rules between them came to a boil. Stefan was
the only man who could nick her temper. "Oh, no. I came
here to say my piece—to set the rules between us." She
hitched up the large traveling tote in front of her, propping
it on her lap for protection. With Stefan, she always felt
very unsafe, and she didn't trust her reaction to him. He
had an easy way of moving around her, as if his body
recognized hers, and all his antennae were focused on her.
"If you're going to stay in Waterville, you'll live by the
rules. You worked on my house and my store, therefore,
you get paid. You can't just run off with me owing you
wages. With that kiss in the field and the town talking, it
will look like I'm paying you with something other than
money."

"I'm staying." Stefan turned a very expensive-looking
pen between his fingers and studied her. "Come here," he
repeated too softly. Then he dropped the pen to the desk
and the metallic click mirrored the warmer one in her
body.

That familiar quiver started deep in Rose's belly, but
she tried to push it away. She glanced at the elegantly
furnished office, the walnut paneling, the leather couches
and chairs, the lush silver carpeting and the skyscraper
view of Chicago burning in the early-afternoon heat. Stefan was a part of all this, not a part of her life. "I can't

play games,'' she whispered, her throat drying as Stefan stood and moved around the desk. ''You belong here, not in Waterville. You'll get bored soon enough, and I can't afford all that sympathy again. I've already gotten one sympathy tuna casserole for losing another chance at marriage. You can't just stir up a town, Stefan. There are consequences.''

Stefan leaned down to pick her up. He carried her to the couch and sat with her in his arms.

''I'm dressed for business,'' Rose said shakily, when she could speak. ''I *mean* business,'' she said in an effort to sound more firm. She sat very straight, her mind blanking as she saw Stefan's dark gaze roaming her body. His finger prowled down her buttoned blouse. ''People will think we're doing something here that we shouldn't be.''

Stefan stroked the side of her throat with his finger and then eased her hair away to nuzzle her skin. ''Shall we?''

''You know that I'm out of that game,'' Rose whispered unevenly as his lips warmed the sensitive skin at the corner of her lips and his fingers began unbuttoning the blouse she wore beneath her jacket.

''I've never been in it—until now,'' Stefan murmured against her throat as his hand slid inside to cup her breast. ''I've missed you.''

Rose tried not to sigh in pleasure, for her body had just remembered everything her mind was telling her not to do. ''If you're trying to soften me up, it's not working.''

''Isn't it?'' Stefan eased away her jacket and her blouse and settled her on the leather couch. She knew she should be saying ''no,'' but her body ached for his touch. His hands trembled as he tore off his own jacket, tie and shirt. That slow, flickering look down her body caught Rose, pinning her.

''It is hot outside,'' she whispered as Stefan slowly lowered himself full-length upon her. He closed his eyes as if drawing pleasure into himself and Rose watched, fascinated. "I've made love before," she said. "It wasn't that good. You wouldn't like it with me. It leaves me all—restless."

Stefan made a growling noise and seemed to shiver. He closed his eyes, groaned and pushed himself upright. He glanced at her, then ran his fingers through his hair. "I promised myself this wouldn't happen. But one look at you and—"

He stared grimly out of the window as if he couldn't bear to look at her. "It's true, then, just like Estelle says. I do not know how to play or to romance. All I want is to be in you, against you, breathing the air you breathe, holding you tight. I sense that if we made love, I would only want you more."

Rose tried to catch her breath. Stefan seemed so vulnerable, so frustrated, and her senses told her to comfort him. She had always been very good at comforting men. She patted his bare, taut shoulder. "You're worried about performing, aren't you? About that too-soon release? You said you hadn't loved anyone since your wife and people say that men lose their edge when they don't keep in practice. It's like any other sport, I suppose. Practice counts."

He glared darkly at her. His words were stiff and grim. "I would hope that I do not have that 'too-soon' problem, and I do not wish to discuss it with you."

She buttoned her blouse and briskly patted his knee. "Well, then. We have other things to discuss, don't we? Before I leave? Like exactly how are we going to deal with the gossip about us? And another thing, I don't like having to run you down to have a conversation about setting the rules between us. Your mother didn't know when you'd be back and she suggested it could be months. *I will not owe you for all that time*. I had to close the store for one whole day to make this trip. I'm going to probably make mistakes on the cash register tomorrow because I'll be tired. Dad and the other men in town are too busy riding their bicycles with your mother. So let's just clean up all the muck and I'll be on my way.''

Stefan's large hand encircled her wrist. ''You're not going anywhere. Do you think I like this…this lack of control with you? With you, it is natural to love. With me, it is difficult to show those feelings and yet, when I see you—touch you—''

''Well,'' Rose said, trying to help Stefan deal with his emotions, ''there are some people who are talkers, and there are others who show their feelings by actions—take for example, how you moved your life to Waterville, to keep your mother and daughter happy.''

She patted his knee again. ''You're a man of action, Stefan, and that might be more important than words. You express yourself in cooking, putting all those tender little touches to the basil leaves and the patés. I'm a fried chicken and potato salad girl and sugar-in-iced-tea myself, but I see how much of yourself you invest in cooking and the presentation. There's always that little flourish, as if you can't resist leaving your work.''

''Always so kind,'' he murmured darkly as he studied her hand on his knee, taking it into his own and placing it over his heart.

The hard beat jarred Rose, traveled straight up her arm and into her body. She stared at him, her senses humming, echoing the heat between them. ''Come up to my apartment, Rose,'' he whispered unevenly. ''We can discuss all this there.''

"Just us?"

He brought her hand up to his lips and sucked her fingers gently. Over their hands, his eyes were dark and soft and warm. "Just us," he repeated huskily.

Six

Stefan watched Rose roam through the modern apartment living room, used for private meetings. He stayed in the corporate building, rather than reopen the Donatien home, because he had every intention of returning to Waterville as soon as his business was finished. In the short time he'd been there, he'd never known such peace, and then there was Rose.

She softened the apartment's sterile decor, her shoulder-length hair catching reddish lights from the sunlight passing through the ceiling-high windows. Always in motion, she touched the sprawling leather couch, skimming her hand over the smooth surface. Everything about her was feminine and graceful and soft. She took in the chrome-framed abstract paintings, and studied the gleaming ultra-modern kitchen. Rose glanced at her wristwatch. "Let's get this over with. I've got a plane to catch and just enough time to tell you off. *Do not come near me with those lips.*"

His lips still tasted of her, his body hardened and ached to hold her long, lithe one close. She'd taken the bait and had come to him. Now he was angry with himself for trying to control her and their relationship. He'd been selfish in his needs, and he didn't like that image of himself; he usually placed his needs after his family's and the business's. "You look tired. Would you like to have a nap before dinner?"

She shook her head. "You're very busy. I won't keep you. And you don't look so hot yourself."

"I have had difficulty sleeping. I missed you. I need you in my bed." He regretted rapping out his emotions as though they were corporate plans. His uncertainty weighed heavily upon him, while his senses told him to go to her, hold her and tell her more gently of the rigid man losing control. Stefan closed his eyes momentarily—*he was feeling delicate, a man awash with frustration, desire and much softer emotions.*

For just a heartbeat, Rose met his intent gaze and then looked away to the city below, a blush quickly rising on her cheeks. "This won't do, Stefan. You can't just tell me things like that."

Of course not. I should have— But in the land of uncertainty, Stefan opted for a direct approach. He had to tell her what he'd done without her leave, and take the consequences. Avenging his lady love's honor was important. "Then you tell me. My daughter tells me that when you were little, you believed in faeries and elves. Think of me as a large elf, happy in my work. But then your ex-fiancés were there, too, weren't they? And the sheriff. Did you offer to pay them?"

"No." Rose turned to him. "Henry and Larry always help. And I help them. That's the way it works. I baby-sit for the sheriff sometimes when he wants a romantic evening with his wife. Most people won't baby-sit for them because their children are pretty inventive. They once handcuffed Mrs. O'Reilly to a rocking chair while she slept…and you're too big to be an elf.''

Stefan took off his suit jacket, placed it over a chair and slid off his tie. He flipped open the top buttons of his shirt and watched Rose. He had to tell her. He took an envelope from the table. ''This is for you. It's the money you paid Mike to start his business.''

Rose blinked and stared blankly at him. ''What?''

''He asked you for money and you gave it to him. Now he has returned it to you.''

Rose sat slowly onto a chair. She gripped her large black tote tightly. ''You saw Mike? Why?''

Once Stefan understood the basics of the encroaching restaurant company, he'd taken a day to deal with Mike. The image of a big man in the greasy, cluttered Ohio garage lined with girlie pictures swept by Stefan. Mike was blond, less than intelligent and far too sure of himself. ''I thought it was best to have a discussion with him.''

''You just went out and found him? *Just like that?*''

Her disbelieving tone deepened Stefan's guilt. He was uncomfortable in relationships and Rose was definitely volatile. He lacked experience in pacifying a woman like Rose. He wanted to sweep her into his arms and take his fill—also, he wanted her to take her fill, as in equal opportunity. He ran his hand through his hair and realized that facing Rose was much more daunting than facing a horde of argumentative business associates. ''I merely visited him. A research agency found him—''

''You hired a private detective?''

Off balance and uncertain now as her eyebrows raised and she placed aside the tote, Stefan nodded grimly. Rose stood and walked across the lush silver carpet to him. She kicked off her shoes and looked up at him. "I said 'why?'"

Stefan looked down at the feminine fist clutching the front of his shirt. He had other intentions for the evening, and at the moment, the path looked rocky. He wasn't backing up— "We had a discussion. He agreed that he had made certain bets about you. He took money from you. I thought your honor needed defending—"

Rose's other fist latched on to Stefan's shirt. She scowled up at him. "I gave him that money to get him out of town. You just take it right back and you apologize."

Stefan shook his head, trying to clear it. "Why would you want him out of town? You were engaged when he left. He ran off with your money."

Rose tried to shake him and failed. "I didn't want to marry him, get it? I just couldn't imagine marriage to Mike. Eventually I saw what he was. He was lazy and he talked too much, and he didn't get along with Dad. In the end, it was just easier giving him money and the idea that Waterville already had too many mechanics. He left because *I* wanted him to. So you've got to apologize and give it back. And what makes you think you've got any right to settle my honor, anyway? I've never been a damsel in distress. I've always managed my own life quite well, without your help."

"You rejected him?" Stefan's mind was whirling. Rose hadn't wanted to marry Mike. "You paid him to leave town?"

Rose tried again to shake Stefan; he stood like a granite boulder. "Even when I caught him with another woman, he still told me he loved me. He was determined to marry me, probably just to prove that he could. I took the easy way out and bribed him with the money I'd saved for that super-duper wedding I'm never going to have. *You have to return it and you have to apologize.* Mike wasn't a bad guy, but he wasn't for me. He's had a hard life and he was sorry about the bet. I think he would have tried to be faithful, even though he might not have been successful. So you just go to him and tell him how sorry you are and give him back the money I gave him.''

Stefan thought of how badly he'd wanted to brawl with Mike after he'd insinuated that Rose was under par as a lover. But Mike hadn't taken Stefan's too quiet invitation. He'd backed off and had taken an hour to get the cash amount. Stefan met Rose's narrowed eyes. ''I do not like orders.''

''You give enough of them. I just watched you course through a meeting like a human shark, tearing apart anything you didn't like. You can't manage lives like you do business, bud.''

Stefan's headache began to throb. He should have known that nothing about Rose was as simple as it seemed. The tag ''bud'' nettled him. He'd wanted her alone, away from interruptions, and he'd maneuvered her into coming to see him. His pride needed one bit of encouragement that she could care for him as he cared for her. Now she was glaring up at him and, once more, he had offended a woman dear to him.

When Rose picked up her tote, preparing to leave, Stefan had to act. He rubbed his chest and wondered how she could have surrendered to him so sweetly just a moment ago and how his plans could go so wrong. It seemed that from the first day he met her, he was making mistakes. He should have known from his experience with his mother and daughter and wife that simplicity wasn't the nature of a woman. He was a man alone, unsteady at the helm of a relationship he wanted very much. He was vulnerable and that made him uneasy. He sorted through his options—what would make Rose want to kiss him again? After a long, deep breath, he reluctantly said, "Very well. If it means so much to you, I will apologize to Mike and give him back the money."

"Thank you," Rose said tightly.

Stefan studied her, the tote gripped tightly in her hands. "Where are you going?"

"Home." The single word sounded like the falling of a tombstone on his plans for a romantic evening with Rose.

"Fine," he said, not wanting to humiliate himself further with her. He'd draw back, consider another approach and wait until she was more receptive to logic.

"Fine," she echoed, meeting his gaze.

The air stilled, quivered and heated between them and each stood perfectly still, Rose clutching her tote. "I'm hungry," she said suddenly and dug inside her bag to retrieve a large homemade cookie. "Granola. Nuts. Raisins. Courtesy of Mrs. Wilkins. She's already warming her oven up for the sympathy dishes. Want one?"

He wanted Rose. "Thanks," he said, his senses heating when her tongue crept out to claim a crumb.

His secretary chose that unfortunate time to put through a call from an irate chef, unhappy with Stefan's decision to revamp the new restaurant's kitchen. The intrusion reminded Stefan that he had little time alone with Rose. "Quit then, if that is what you want. All your specialty dishes are the property of Donatien Restaurants—I taught them to you—they are recipes that have been in my family for generations. You will have to develop complete new ones, if you work elsewhere."

Stefan punched the intercom button to Megan, his secretary. "I told you to hold all calls. One more and there goes your Christmas bonus."

Megan was silent in the way that meant she was not pleased. He regretted speaking sharply to a woman he respected. He trusted her logical decisions as to the importance of calls. An irate chef could cause bad publicity for Donatien's and she had been right to put through the call. Ordinarily Stefan would have called her back and thanked her. Business and his relationship with Rose were not compatible ingredients. "I apologize, Megan. I am under stress," he admitted. "You are very efficient and I am grateful for your help. Your bonus is intact. You were right to put through this call. Thank you."

Tonight, however, he wanted no interruptions. Rose eyed him as he took the cookie, automatically assessing the ingredients. "You're having a bad day, aren't you?"

He'd had a bad two weeks without her, but a man's pride would only let him say so much. "Yes."

He caught Rose's soft, motherly look and tossed it away. He wanted her all-woman look, the one that said he wasn't a "bud." "But spare me the sympathy."

They ate the cookies and Rose studied him. "You've got that little-boy look again. If you're doing it on purpose, it's a killer. You're pouting, aren't you?"

"Mike is a lowlife," Stefan muttered. "I do not pout."

"You didn't hurt him, did you?" she asked worriedly. "He talks like he's tough, but he's really not in shape. Even I could take him in a wrestling match. In fact I did. He's big and slow. I pinned him in ten seconds."

Stefan did not like the low growl that was his own. In his mind he was tearing Mike from Rose and challenging him to a duel at dawn, in the fog-draped trees. "When are you returning?"

She glanced at the big chrome clock on the wall. "In about five hours."

Five hours alone with Rose could be heaven. Stefan's

hopes lifted. Perhaps he could correct the errors he had made with her. "Have dinner with me?"

She shrugged. "Okay, but if it's too much trouble, the sandwiches at the vending machines in the airport are fine." She smiled at his grimace.

Later, after a fried chicken and potato salad meal, she sipped her iced tea—just perfect, the way she liked it, with sugar added to the pitcher. "I didn't know dinner was going to be here, in your apartment. You're pretty good at home cooking. This is quite a meal for late afternoon."

"Nothing to it. A simple meal." Stefan did not want to tell her that he'd salvaged time from his tightly packed days to prepare the same dinner for his staff. He'd kept chicken and potatoes on hand every day, just waiting for Rose to appear. He'd noted the staff's comments and adjusted from his first failures. He also noted that Rose was in a better mood, because she had a loving heart and once she'd said her piece, she was ready to move on.

Stefan was also ready to move on—straight into making love with her. His body told him that lovemaking would seal and settle their future, that all else would fall into place after the event. His logic told him to move slowly, carefully with Rose, to obtain her in the most gentlest of ways, to make certain that she received her due as a well-loved woman. "Let's move to the couch," he suggested. "You must have had a long day. Let me rub your feet."

The road to desire started with her toes and insoles, Rose decided twenty minutes later as she lay on the couch—and the path wound upward. With soft music playing, Stefan's big, warm hands on her feet, and the good meal filling her, she was ready for more dessert than the rest of the cookies. Sitting on the couch, Stefan had that appealing, male-at-home look, his shirt opened to show that fascinating wedge of hair on his chest. She studied his expression, that infinite concentration as his hands moved carefully over her, massaging her feet in his lap. She'd seen him in action, laying out the foundation for acquiring a new company, curtly itemizing the changes that needed to be made, the contract clauses that needed defining. He'd methodically ripped through a mountain of decisions, slashing his signature on paperwork at the same time. Rose had listened to his voice very carefully; not once did his voice lower and that seductive accent appear.

Yet she had known that every moment, he was aware of her. Those darkened eyes had periodically pinned her. His smile was brief and pleased, before he cruised into the business meeting like a warlord moving through battle. The intensity of that knowledge had shocked her. Once, while he was pacing, wrapped in the business takeover and staff changes, he had stopped those curt, one-two-three sentences and touched her hair. He had lifted it to the light and smiled tenderly at her. "Catch any pigs lately?" he'd asked huskily as his accent curled intimately around her.

Everyone in the room had studied her critically, the woman who had Stefan Donatien's attention. "One or two," she'd answered, because she'd been in charge of the children's greased pig contest at the town fair.

He'd run a fingertip across her cheeks and the bridge of her nose, and smiled softly at the other businesspeople in the room. "She has freckles. I think they are kisses from faeries. Isn't Rose beautiful?" he'd noted softly, in the slight accent that said his emotions were touched. Then he had stroked her hair once and turned back to business as if it were never interrupted…as if she weren't blushing and everyone in the room smiling knowingly at her. They had been good, warm, honest smiles, as if they were pleased that Stefan was pleased.

She frowned now, listening to Stefan's low, rumbling voice. "I will apologize. I will apologize. I will be sweet."

"I do appreciate you trying," she said, smiling at him and realizing how difficult the apology would be for him. It seemed very natural to sit up and tug his head closer to kiss his cheek. "I forgive you for not answering my telephone call, and you'll take the wages, of course. I know they are only a pittance compared to what you earn, but my pride is important to me."

Stefan nodded, and watched her in that dark, smoldering way. "I have not entertained another woman in this apartment," he stated quietly. "In many ways, you are the first for me."

"I think—" Rose inhaled and closed her eyes, because Stefan's soft, tempting kiss had stopped all her thoughts. She jerked back the hand she had just slid inside his shirt to smooth that wonderful chest.

He turned slightly, kissed the side of her mouth and then the other. He pressed her hand over his heart. "Did you miss me?"

"Yes," she whispered against his lips, mentally scolding herself for dropping into the danger zone with him. The taste of him filled her, throbbed low in her body, rocketed through her like a heat-seeking missile. She realized dimly that she was bending over him, and Stefan was really only responding to *her* kisses—she was seeking him, her arms around him. His head lay back on the cushion, and she was definitely making all the moves.

Rose, the adventuress, wanted him. Rose, the woman who had been hurt, feared coming too close—and then Stefan's hands began to smooth her body and with a sigh, she gave herself to the pleasure. She feared the tenderness she felt for Stefan, more than a physical need.

She feared trusting him, and yet she sensed that Stefan

wouldn't hurt her, that he would be very protective and safe.

She feared "safe."

"I'm not too certain about this," she said in an attempt to be logical. Despite her will, her body was coming to life, pounding with the need to make up for all those lonely, restless nights.

"Well, then," he murmured against her throat. "I am. Continue, please…if you wish, that is."

The formal phrase pleased her because Stefan was very affected by her. Men normally weren't; excitement brewed within her. Was it possible that she could seduce Stefan? Heat shimmered through him, she could feel his heart racing against her hand. The hard texture of a male nipple etched her palm. And yet, Stefan held very still, a vein in his temple throbbing. She kissed his temple, wanting to soothe him. In the taste of Stefan's skin, in the beat of his heart, she found pleasure she had never experienced. When she'd made love with Mike, it was an experiment with a novelty—to test herself and see if she were still "womanly," and it was over very quickly. She sensed that Stefan would linger and savor and pleasure and be very thorough.

"I regret—" Stefan tensed as she kissed his throat. "I regret that I am sometimes grim and formal. It is not because I do not feel, it is because—"

"I know," she whispered softly, allowing her tongue to flick that dark, wonderful texture of his jaw. She shook when she saw his hand enclose her breast and cuddle it gently. He eased the fabric aside and studied the creamy mound, and his body vibrated with the tension racking hers. His eyes closed momentarily as if he were taking the sight into him to hoard. The sight of him so pleasured, so engrossed in her body, enchanted Rose.

Rose-who-feared knew she should be listening to reason—that Stefan wasn't meant to live in small rural towns like Waterville, and she couldn't think of living anywhere else. She should be thinking about how she'd feel when he left. But she wasn't—because right now, he looked too delicious to resist. Like a great big package that just needed unwrapping to discover the good stuff inside.

"Be careful," he whispered as she moved to sit on his lap and stroke his hair. She'd wanted to do that since that night he held her when she cried. She wanted those strong, safe arms around her. "You think you will have me and fly away home, don't you?" he asked unevenly and eased away from her.

He stood, ran a trembling hand through his hair, and walked to a small cabinet. He opened it and poured a small amount of wine into an elegant glass. He swirled the drink and shook his head. "I have feelings for you. They are deeper than a momentary feeding of needs. I think if I took you quickly, you might excuse that passion as an impulse, some indulgence between flights. I want you to be very certain about me, that it is not only a seduction I wish, but also a relationship. I do not wish to be considered a 'bud.' Therefore, I think it best to adjourn."

Rose's heart flip-flopped and fell into anger. She stood and straightened her clothing, her hands shaking. "You could at least drop the business language at a moment like this."

"It is how I speak when deeply affected. I apologize. How little would it mean, if we were to hurriedly make love. I would feel used, a sexual object, rather than a companion of the heart. You would be able to justify your actions as a weakness you indulged and regretted. You would have to comfort me, because you have a soft heart and do not wish to wound anyone, and then I might misinterpret that kindness and make love to you again, and then our roles would become a habit. Each of us might be uncertain of the whys and hows of the true relationship. I wish no regrets on either of our parts. If you wish to rest in my bed, I will not bother you. But I would like to lie beside you. In bed. With my clothes on. Without touching you.'' Stefan's deep voice was uneven, his body tense as he spoke. ''I would wish to touch you, of course, to hold you close and naked against me—but it is not time yet.''

''You're not in control of this situation, you know,'' she said unevenly, images of Stefan's tall muscled body tangled with hers stunning her. He'd be all rumpled and cuddly and magnificent. ''It's a share-and-share-alike deal. And we're not on a specified schedule.''

He nodded grimly. ''I must make certain that you know my intentions are not frivolous. Base rules are always a necessity. I would not like to immediately hit a home run and then lose the game. It would be like taking a soufflé too soon from the oven.''

Rose threw up her hands. For the first time in her life, she'd wanted to fly from her safe anchors and Stefan had just rejected her attempt at seduction. ''Well, you have me there!''

Because tears were burning her lids, she hurried into the bathroom. She tried for composure and failed. Finally, emotionally drained, she opened the door to find Stefan leaning against the wall. His expression was grim, lines of fatigue showing in his face. ''Rose?''

With as much dignity as she could manage, Rose walked to the bed and lay down stiffly. After a moment, she curled on her side, tears flowing down her cheeks. She was exhausted from nights of wondering about Stefan, if he'd had a lover since they'd kissed, if he'd missed her, if she could trust her heart again. Some hidden place inside her had wanted him to make love to her quickly, to ease that empty, aching void, if only momentarily. *She'd offered herself to him, and he'd refused.* So much for her appeal to men, even ones proclaiming to need her in their bed. Nothing was safe anymore, not with Stefan. She'd rest and then she'd face reality. "I'm just tired. I'll rest a moment and then I'll be on my way."

The large bed sagged slightly and she heard Stefan's deep, ragged sigh behind her. "You're tired, too. It's okay. Lie down. I won't jump you," she murmured.

His big, warm body curled around hers, spoon-fashion. He nuzzled her hair and smoothed it away from her nape. "You're too tired. You could stay. You could fly back later," he whispered against her throat.

"Is that an invitation?" she asked, already beginning to slide into sleep. Stefan pulled her back against him, his hand cupping her breast. The gesture seemed so natural that Rose placed her hand over his. "Yes, I missed you," she whispered sleepily, drained by travel and emotion.

"Mmm," Stefan murmured as if deeply pleased. He gathered her closer and gently pulled her hips back against him, his hand sweeping over her stomach and lower on her thighs, then returning upward over her hip to recapture her breast. "That is a good sign. Are you staying?"

"No. I'm going back to Waterville where it's safe and I know the rules. Make certain I don't miss my flight at nine. I've got to open the store in the morning. Dad has taken up a morning exercise routine and it's really good for him." Then Rose gave herself to the gentle caress of his hands. Later, she would remember turning to Stefan. She would remember his indrawn breath when she flung her arms around him, her leg wrapping around his long ones and his body trembling as he drew her against him. She'd hovered there for a heartbeat, thinking of how sweetly he held her when he could have taken her so easily. The rocking of his body was not that of desire, but rather of a companion giving comfort. She would remember feeling safe with Stefan.

Hours later, Stefan watched Rose board her plane, the night wind whipping at her hair, the floodlights outlining her willowy, tall body. In their goodbye, she'd held him close and tight, her body shaking. She held him as if he were an anchor in a changing, dangerous sea. Rose's fatigue had opened an insight to why she feared a relationship. She hadn't wanted marriage, not deep down inside, where the scars still bled. Rose smiled and laughed and warmed hearts, but she feared loving too deeply. He wondered if she knew how she had cried out in her sleep, ''Mommy, you said you loved me. Why did you leave?''

The second week of July, Stefan clamped his lips closed against comments about Estelle's driving. She had picked him up at the airport in Kansas City, and had driven him straight to the rolling green hills surrounding Waterville. The long drive helped him adjust to the change from city to country, to the slower pace of small, rural towns. Slower loving, slower kisses with Rose, Stefan thought.

''I've signed up for the fall semester at the local college,'' Estelle was saying. ''If you and Grandmother move back to Chicago, I can stay in a dorm or rent an apartment. And Rose said if that is the case, I can always come home and stay with her when I can. Do you know that as loving as she is, she doesn't have one pet? Not one. She's got a houseful of plants and talks to them like they were alive, but she doesn't want a pet. How do you figure that?''

''I imagine she feels she's too busy at the store,'' Stefan said, studying the tall oaks that would turn fiery in the autumn. He sensed that Rose didn't want the attachment for fear of losing something...someone that she loved. Her nightmare had been revealing; Rose basically didn't trust life—or Stefan.

He'd worked long hours getting the new restaurant incorporated into Donatien's chain. It was uniquely decorated, while its dishes retained the fine quality of his other restaurants. He had spent a whole day with the disgruntled chef, smoothing his ruffled pride. Rose with her ability to make people comfortable could have done it in ten minutes. Stefan was exhausted, but now he was coming home to his fields and barn and life away from chef-stealing businesses. His daughter was blooming, her tales of country life running from one into another. "I will cook dinner for your friends," he offered. "You can watch movies at our home. I think your grandmother and I will probably stay on the farm. I may have to return to the city, now and then, for business, but from her calls, she is quite happy."

Estelle looked at Stefan, her hair flying away from her face as she gripped the steering wheel of her small red compact truck. "Daddy, you don't need to cook for my friends. Please...I mean, there is no reason to go to so much work. After all, you've got Rose to think of now. You need to cook for her."

Stefan reeled from Estelle's statement. He had called Rose, but the telephone lines between them were frustrating and he regretted sounding so curt. He sensed that if she were in his arms, he could be more relaxed. "What do you mean, I have 'Rose to think of now?' Has she said something?"

Estelle lifted an eyebrow. "She misses you and you know it."

Stefan's exhausted senses awakened, surging to life. He barely noticed Mrs. Wilkins's smiling face and waving hand. He returned the wave automatically. "Glad you're back, sonny!" she called. "Come over to my house anytime. Never seen Rose in such a stew."

But Stefan was too wrapped in Estelle's "Rose-comment" to be stunned by the older woman's sudden enthusiasm for him. *"She said that?"*

"A woman can tell, Daddy. It's how she looked after her visit with you, as if she wasn't quite certain. Rose is always certain of everything. And the way she talks about you like this—'arrogant, macho, beast, hard-to-get, low-down, hunk, righteous, uptight, crappie-stealing, gorgeous.' When I asked if she'd heard from you, she glared at me. So I know that something is cooking between you two. You know, you could call and talk a little, you know, sexy—if you know how—to her. I hope you didn't talk in that stiff way—that business way that you use when you're deeply touched."

Estelle reached to tug his tie. "I love you, Daddy, but please don't try to cook for my friends."

The third week of July, Waterville buzzed about the watermelon-eating and the seed-spitting contests, and about Rose making mistakes at the paint store. She wasn't in a good mood, the gossips said, and Stefan Donatien was the reason. For his part, Stefan was picking carefully through his decision to wait for Rose's heart. Business at night and day farmwork helped relieve his body's tension, but his mind ran on to sweeter things—like how she lay beside him, all fragrant and soft and cuddly. Like how, in her sleep, she'd turned to him, thrown her arms around him, snuggled her face against his throat and had latched one long leg over his as if preventing him from escaping. The incredible tenderness he'd felt for her at that moment had stunned him. He'd lain very still for a moment, her easy breath sweeping across his throat and then it was only natural for him to give her comfort, to rock her. The pleasure was in giving to Rose when she needed him.

Stefan cherished that memory while he considered how to make his next move. He wanted it to be well-planned, so that his words flowed smoothly for her.

He didn't have to make that move, because the next day he was alone, on top of the barn. He worked to straighten the old copper rooster weather vane. Below him, Rose's pickup shot like a bullet over the curved road shaded with oaks. She had given him just one week before she came calling. It had taken all of his strength not to see her, to touch her, to call her, but Rose didn't trust him now—not enough to openly share her nightmares with him. That slight bruise had hurt—that she didn't trust him. With trust as a missing ingredient in their relationship, the future would always be threatened.

Now, with Rose's pickup skidding to a stop in his driveway, Stefan shook his head. Behind the windshield, her expression was similar to his mother's, when she decided to clean house and let nothing stop her. He was without the protection of his mother's smoothing grace and his daughter's lighthearted conversation. Estelle was at work at the hamburger drive-in and Yvette was at a church social. Later, she would stay with the widow Harris for "girl talk" and Estelle would stay overnight with her friends. Everyone in his home had a social life but himself, Stefan brooded, and admitted that his body was already humming at the sight of Rose.

He studied the way she slammed her pickup door and headed for the house, before she saw him up on the old barn's roof. "I want to talk with you," she called as she started toward him. Her tone said she was not happy; her frown said lightning bolts were about to strike. Stefan could almost hear the rumble of thunder. He could feel the excitement that Rose always created, simmering inside him.

He descended the ladder and Rose stopped in front of him. Her eyes widened as she looked at him, her gaze tracing his hair, his cheeks and lips and throat and bare chest and all the way down his legs. "You're all sweaty," she whispered in a husky, sensual way that dried his throat.

Stefan couldn't move. Every part of him wanted to snare her close and feed upon her, to carry her into the barn and— But that was not his intention on his way to understand Rose's needs. "Of course. If you wish, you may wait while I shower. Then we can talk."

He added a shrug to appear casual, when his senses were racing. "Then perhaps I could cook for you. It is almost time for dinner and my family will be away for the night. It would be very nice to talk with you."

"A shower?" she repeated in a tone that unnerved him. "Yes, I think I'd like that."

In the shower, working hurriedly, Stefan reconsidered her words. Of course, she meant that he needed a shower; he had obviously misinterpreted her statement. He quickly ran through his planned talk with her—about how he knew that trust was difficult for her, but that he would cherish her and never do anything to make her feel less than safe. He would tell her he understood about her fears and how she had talked in her sleep; he would tell how he knew that her pain from her mother's desertion was unresolved and sometimes pain had no easy closure.

Then he weighed not discussing her mother and Rose's fears of safety and stepped from the shower, drying and wrapping a towel around his waist. How could he explain to her that on a primitive level, he sensed she was the other part of his heart, his body? If she was wary of a deep relationship, a commitment to a love, that might frighten her even more.

Crossing the hallway from the bathroom to his bedroom, he saw Rose standing in the living room. And then she turned to find him in the hallway and he stopped, pinned by Rose's sultry expression, the way she seemed to soften as she studied him through the shadows. He made no effort to hide the hardening of his body, though he feared the obvious beneath his towel might shock her. In that moment, as natural as sunrise and spring rain and the dark secret night, they were nothing but a man and a woman, without the years of complications between them.

"I hadn't planned on you, or feeling like this," Rose whispered so quietly it rocked his soul. "I'm terrified, but I want you."

"I do not see this as a problem, because I want you, too," he answered slowly, but with all his heart.

"What shall we do?"

"I think we should explore all possibilities, *ma chérie*."

Seven

Rose's heart pounded as Stefan walked down the hallway to her, a tall man whose shoulders filled the narrow space. He moved sleekly, gracefully toward her, the dim light skimming over his powerful body. In a suit, he looked hard and chiseled and cold, but with only a towel around his narrow hips, he bore a primitive warrior look as if his time had come to take what he wanted.

Rose couldn't move, pinned by the sight, his muscles flowing beneath that dark skin, that wedge of hair on his chest, droplets gleaming there. He came to stand near her, framing her face with his large, rough hands. In his eyes, she saw a reflection of her desire; it sparkled in the beads of water on his shoulders, in his waving hair. He lowered his head to hers, placing his lips exactly so on hers. Then he studied her so closely she thought he could see the fears and shadows she didn't want exposed. ''I didn't expect you in my life, either," he whispered. "Are you certain you want to make love with me?"

"If you're feeling up to it," she returned unevenly, shivering as she controlled her need to wrap her arms around him.

His smile was soft and tender, his gaze searching her face. "It has been so long since I've first wanted you. That first need to make love to you has grown with each day. In my lifetime, I have never wanted another woman like I want you."

She hovered between the fear and the need for Stefan. "No inconvenience then?"

"None at all. In fact, it will be a pleasure," he returned softly. With that, Stefan gently lifted her in his arms. It seemed so natural to settle against him, to place her head on his shoulder. His heart pounded heavily, safely, as he carried her up the stairs. She hadn't realized how powerful he was, how hot his skin was beneath her lips, how strong that vein in his throat pounded as he carried her into a large room, starkly masculine and uncluttered.

The setting sun slid through the windows, laying gentle stripes across the heavy wooden furniture, books stacked on the night table beside the sturdy, big bed. Browns and tans mixed with the sheen of the wooden floor, broken only by a rectangular cream rug. On the tall, old dresser, bold with its antique metal knobs and pulls, lay his trappings for business—his expensive gold watch, a flat wallet, his compact cellular phone. Framed pictures of his family stood nearby. On the outside door of the closet hung two suits, a gray and a black, a tie hung round the hanger of a pristine white shirt. Nearby were his dress shoes, the Italian leather polished, almost mirrorlike. His work books, with leather lace, stood by worn running shoes. Jeans, pressed with a crease were folded over the back of a big chair, and a stack of folded T-shirts rested neatly on the seat.

Holding her, Stefan breathed quietly, his body tense. She sensed that this was important to him, bringing her to his bed, a ritual that was both beautiful and terrifying. There in the dark planes of his face, he shielded his emotions, as though giving her time to deny what had begun.

Rose closed her eyes, taking in the moment, dissecting it. Long ago, she dreamed of a man carrying her just like this, of making her feel feminine and desired. She smoothed his damp shoulder, admiring the beauty of the powerful planes, the tense cords and muscles shifting beneath that wonderful tanned skin. The soft light of evening spread gently into the room, filling her heart with peace. Somehow, a part of her always knew that Stefan would be very courtly, very gentle with her.

He placed her on her feet and traced her flushed face with his fingertip, tilting her chin up for another intense study as he waited for her to tell him this was what she wanted, to let her decide. Rose stood very still, then let her hands speak for her, smoothing his shoulders, his throat and latching in his hair. "Yes," she whispered, drawing him down for her kiss.

She hadn't expected the heat, the sudden storm as Stefan trembled and opened her lips with his, his intimate kiss searching and pleasuring. She heard the tear of cloth and knew that he was as eager as she, and that pleasured her more. The seductress rose in her, slipping from her lifetime hiding place, as she skimmed his body with her hands, over that flat stomach and lower and up to flatten on those sliding muscles of his back. They quivered to her caress, exciting her because she knew that his body was susceptible to her touch, reacting almost as if the leashes of his control were slipping. The temptation to tear away those tethers circled her, for she had never played at lovemaking, and in comparison, her one experience had seemed sterile and without emotion, a mechanical disaster that left her unsatisfied.

She sensed deep inside, where all her fears lay quivering, that Stefan would not use her quickly and for his pleasure alone. He was too thorough, too thoughtful and considerate. She gently nipped his lip and enjoyed his suddenly indrawn breath, the shock and the surprise heightening the passion between them. Her blouse and bra came away, carelessly tossed by Stefan onto a chair. He eased her body against his, looking down to where her breasts nestled against his chest. He had that same fierce look she remembered, as if he would struggle against his own primitive desires to please her, yet the sight of her breasts, small and pale against him, seemed to intensify his need.

His hands were at her stomach now, shaking, hurrying to unbutton the snaps of her denim shorts. They slid from her and Stefan's touch roamed her bottom, before sliding inside, tugging away her briefs. And there in the cool, dark room, he held her away from him as he roughly stripped the towel between them, and slowly, so slowly fitted her body to his. The brand of his desire nudged her, and Rose stood still as the shocking warmth spread within her, the softening and opening.

''Rose....'' he whispered unevenly as his hands caressed and seduced and prowled intimately lower. The clean sheets on his bed smelled like sunshine and wind as he settled her upon it. Lying beside her, Stefan tugged her against him, and Rose quickly caught him with her arms and legs.

He momentarily stiffened with the gentle attack, then began to smile. It was a confident, devastating, tender smile that warmed and softened his face. "That's it. Hold me, Rose."

For an instant, she regretted her action, a strong athlete claiming a prize, rather than a woman softly welcoming a man to her. But Stefan's smile said he was pleased.

It would be no gentle journey, she knew, for the need to devour him, to pleasure him rose too sharply within her. He came slowly upon her, pushed back a bit to study her in the shadows, his expression honed and tense before he kissed her throat, her breasts. She cried out, vibrating with excitement and pleasure, as he suckled gently there, pleasuring her. She couldn't lie still, her body undulating, aching. Then, after reaching for protection, Stefan settled firmly over her with the caress of his hand sweeping her body, her thigh.

The nudge of his desire caused her to tense and Stefan paused as she adjusted, waiting for her. Their gazes locked, he began the sensual journey, entering her so gently that she cried out at the beauty.

She shivered and gripped his arms, her fingers digging in to hold him as the sensations of fullness riveted her.

He lay quietly, locked inside her, watching her, holding himself slightly away. He studied her flushed face, her shielded eyes, the lips that had opened for his. "I dreamed of you like this—warm and soft and fragrant, tight and damp and—"

Rose shook beneath him, her hips arching, her body taut and she closed her eyes as she sealed in the first rippling pleasure. When she opened her eyes, Stefan had begun to move gently, the rhythm so timeless she met and drifted in it, locking her gaze with his. Then suddenly, deep inside, the pounding, flashing heat would not be denied and she tightened around Stefan, meeting his feverish kisses, digging her fingers in to hold him just there. The riveting flash and thunder struck within her, she realized slowly as Stefan's body stiffened, and there on that silvery, glittering plane, time waited and yet ran on in waves of pleasure.

He breathed unevenly, coming slowly down to settle against her, to hold her tight in the aftermath of that heat as her racing heart slowed, her breast against him quivering. His hands skimmed over her, defining the softness and the curves, caressing them lazily.

She wanted to talk, to tell him that now she knew—that now she knew what? How wonderful a caring man could be, a tender man? That she was woman and soft and melting and happy and…in the end, Rose settled against Stefan, wrapping her arm and leg around his so he couldn't leave her. She drifted in the peace running through her, one she'd never enjoyed. Peace…whatever had been wrong in her life was now right, at least for the moment.

Then Stefan was kissing her again, his warm body seeking hers, filling her and suddenly she was flying and happy and hungry for him….

Rose awoke in the morning, her arms and legs tangled with Stefan's heavily muscled ones, his heart beating slowly beneath her cheek. She breathed quietly, adjusting to the bold light skimming into the window and the icy slash of fear, the past churned and stormed and caught her.

She could ruin both of their lives, the dark shadows chasing her.

Her muscles ached slightly, her body tingling now, and she fought the tears behind her lids. He was already too close, and he wouldn't be sent away so easily.

That afternoon, while repairing the barn's stall, Stefan damned himself for his hunger, for his need of Rose. He'd taken her twice in the night and once almost before she awoke. No considerate lover would initiate his sweetheart so quickly—in one night—especially when she was so tight and new— Stefan held very still in the silence of the barn, the kittens mewing in their mother's nest. His mind flashed back to that tightness, to Rose's surprise, and he damned himself again. Whatever sex Rose may have had, it wasn't with a demanding lover who also gave her pleasure. Her blush this morning, her hurried, flustered exit from his bed, leaving her bra and briefs behind, wasn't that of an experienced woman. Stefan scrubbed his hands over his face, and shook his head. He'd wanted to say so much, but his body and heart had taken control. So much for a man, powerful in business and helpless in love— *love?*

Of course he loved her. Who wouldn't? The whole town loved Rose Granger, a tall, fresh-faced woman with a beautiful, caring heart and a dazzling smile. They were a part of her life, just as she was of theirs. She was probably having a difficult time this morning, and seeing him might only disturb her. Stefan decided that the next time he saw Rose, he was going to draw upon whatever charm he could manage and tell her—what? In his stiff, rigid way when he was affected by his emotions, he could hurt her. But the next time, Stefan promised himself, he would not make love to her until she knew how much he cared. He should try that sexy telephone talk Estelle recommended. He should call Rose—it was almost quitting time and only hours since she'd awakened in a tangle of sheets and had blown the strand of hair from her face.

Stefan smiled wistfully. She'd looked like a faerie, all rosy and warm and tousled in his bed, bewildered as she slowly awoke to him. He frowned then, remembering her sharp knee as she quickly crossed him, scrambling on her way to the floor on the other side. Just awakened and rudely so, he wasn't exactly happy, his unique ache not the one he had planned, as she hurriedly tugged on her clothing and muttered about being late to open the store. Stefan was still recovering when the front door had slammed behind her. Her pickup had skidded out of his driveway, hitting the already crooked post once more. Rose's expression had been that of fear and shock and because of that, he'd decided to give her time to resolve what had happened between them.

She wasn't afraid of him; she'd come too freely to him, opened for him. Yet another fear held her, that of loving and losing.

He watched his mother in her vegetable garden, the sound of her happy humming carried to him by the gentle summer breeze. Yvette snipped her roses and began filling her basket. When Stefan finished hammering the last board into the repaired stall, he had sorted his priorities for dealing with his long-term Rose-relationship. He would make her comfortable with him—how could he do that when his body ached for hers so passionately? Would she ever trust him enough to share her heartbreak?

He rubbed his forehead. If he were better at relationships, his words more smoothly crafted, he might be able to open the shadows she guarded so fiercely. They slithered between a complete relationship and full trust. Rose's pain wasn't something he could lay out as he might a problem on the business table.

Last night, one look from Rose and he had been stirred into desire that he couldn't waylay. He looked at the bouquet of summer flowers his mother had stuck in front of his face. "Go to her," Yvette ordered softly, an understanding, tender smile upon her face.

"Everybody knows," Rose whispered urgently as she sat across the café booth from Stefan. She held the bouquet tightly against her, not yielding it to Peggy the waitress to place in water. "Don't ask me how, they just know you and I...*you know.*"

Stefan smiled as he studied the café's menu. He didn't want to tell Rose that her expression hid little, that she glowed. Everyone in Waterville knew Rose's very open expressions and when she was distracted and by what—rather, by whom. He was quite happy with that rosy glow, because it meant he had succeeded in giving her pleasure that wasn't easily forgotten. Rose's flustered expression when seeing him at the store's closing time had shifted into a sensually hungry look. Stefan inhaled slowly; life was good. With Rose as a dinner enchantress, all rosy and warm and flustered and nervous of him, he could tolerate whatever the cook could serve.

"You're not picking at the food," Rose noted as they ate.

"It's good," Stefan returned lightly. "Filling, nutritious, fresh vegetables—a bit overcooked, but good."

"Doesn't it bother you?" she asked, leaning across the booth's table to whisper to him. She glanced at Danny, whose hands were on his generous hips, his eyes narrowed on Stefan.

"Mmm." Stefan scanned the small, comfortable café. He smiled at Danny and gave him a thumbs-up sign. After a warning frown, Danny shifted his three-hundred-pound bulk back into the shadows of the kitchen. Locals were enjoying familiar fare, dining and talking and sliding searching glances at Rose and himself.

Rose's foot came up to nudge him. "Stefan. Doesn't it bother you that they're looking at us, and what they must be thinking?"

He captured that slender foot, and surprised himself by grinning and slipping off her shoe. Her eyes darkened immediately when he caressed her foot, bringing it to his lap. Her eyes widened, her hand trembled and her water glass spilled. She hurriedly plucked napkins and covered the ice. Her smile at the waitress who came to clean away the mess was shaky. "Nice touch, Donatien," sixty-year-old Suzie murmured with a wink. "You can do my feet anytime."

"I am certain they are quite lovely."

"*Stefan!*" Rose said in a hushed tone after Suzie left with a knowing giggle. "You can't just do things like that."

He released her foot and took her hand, toying with it. "I would like to have you for dessert," he said quietly and enjoyed her rising blush. "No one eats pie like you, sliding it from the tip of your fork into your mouth. Closing your eyes as you take the pleasure into you—"

Rose blinked and her mouth parted and moved as if she were trying to speak and couldn't. She swallowed finally and managed unevenly, "I've got plans for tonight. And you're not them. I'm going to take a long bath and read updates on the paint catalogs and—"

"I held a faerie in my arms last night," Stefan heard himself say quietly. "I would very much like to hold her now and taste the unique flavor of her desire—"

Rose's delicate shudder said his statement had had the impact he'd sought and meant. "I think we should leave," she said breathlessly. "People are staring and you can't talk like that here."

"So proper," he teased, enjoying himself, feeling very young and carefree and reckless. "What did you come to see me about last night? Before we were…distracted?"

"I forget. But I remember it wasn't good. You've got to go home now, and I've got to go to my house, before…you know," she said urgently as she watched him bring her palm to his lips to kiss the center.

"Why?"

"You know," she said more urgently.

"Can't you be trusted?" He almost released his laughter, the joy warming him. He wondered when he had enjoyed life so freely and the answer came back—never.

"Not with you," she answered as if the words were dragged out of her. The admission was enough to soothe whatever doubts Stefan had about her attraction to him. Flirtation was new to him and he reveled in his success.

"You're leering. Men do not leer or look steamy and all revved up at me. It has to do with my low sexuality," Rose said darkly as she stood, holding her bouquet close to her.

"That has been disproved quite efficiently, I believe," Stefan returned and watched her rising blush. Then because nothing else would do, and because Stefan had definite delicious proof that he wasn't in Rose's "bud bin," he swept her into his arms. He bent her back, crushing the flowers between them and kissed her as his hunger demanded.

A half hour later, Rose broke her silence with a curt, "When they started cheering, you didn't have to take a bow. Arrogant, full of yourself, crappie-catching, lip nibbling— The next thing you know, they'll be watching *us* instead of television soaps."

He studied how sweet she looked, framed in the cab of his old beloved pickup. "You're quite enchanting when you're in a snit."

"I don't do 'snits.'" She bashed him with the bouquet and petals flew fragrantly into the air, reminding him of the scent of her body.

She studied him, silence within his pickup quivering louder than the evening crickets and frogs along the lake. "You're all warmed up right now, aren't you?"

"Did you think last night was all there was between us?" He carefully took the battered bouquet from her and placed it on his dashboard. Rose inhaled sharply, and his gaze jerked down to the nipples pushed against her T-shirt. "Yes, I want you," he admitted, his mouth aching to taste her.

"Men don't usually come back for a second helping."

Stefan brought her hand to his lips, kissing her fingers. He studied her before stating gently, "You are not an experienced woman. Your body says more than your words."

She shivered, closing her eyes. "Just once. I gave myself to that stupid idiot because I thought that would make everything right. It didn't. It hurt and he fell asleep right away."

Stefan wished he could see Mike once more—the mechanic needed lessons in consideration. Stefan had little time for anger in his life, plowing through it with schedules and demands, but now it flamed inside him. "You're right. He was an idiot. Not worth a moment's thought. Discard the incident. It never happened."

"You think so?"

"Erase it. You should know how attractive and desirable you are. How natural and sweet and feminine. You're a perfect jewel, a dewdrop on the soft petal of a rose. Only a fool would let you slip away." Stefan wanted to give her more than the truth in his words, but they were the best he could manage without getting into his rigid-emotional mode. He put his arm around her and drew her close to him, nuzzling her hair. He smiled softly into it— he felt as if all the pieces in his life were placed together at the moment—a man, his beloved pickup, his love sitting close to him in the night while the moon rose over the lake. Its silvery trail slid amid the lilies where the faeries slept curled and safe.

Then Rose lifted her face, studied him and placed her hand along his cheek to draw him down for a short, light kiss. "You're basically a nice man, Stefan. I don't regret making love with you."

"No?" he managed to say as he reveled in the sense that Rose thought well of him. "I thought it was an especially nice occurrence."

She laughed knowingly then, an enchanting, husky laughter that was more like music. The next thing Stefan realized after a clumsy scuffle on the front seat, in which his tall body demanded that the door be opened, while his hand found Rose's breast, was that he was lying beneath her. "You're an unusual man, Stefan Donatien. You try very hard to smooth the rough edges of life. I heard how you donated money for the school's playground and for the town library, and how you've been helping the elderly whose pensions don't meet their medical expenses. Yvette asked me to suggest names and said that she was acting on your orders, paying bills they couldn't. You've got a good heart, too," she noted raggedly before she came down upon him in a storm of quick, hungry kisses.

Dazed and floating in pleasure, Stefan forgot notions of a proper bed and how respectable lovers acted who were his age. His hands roamed up her shorts and found the petals of Rose's desire. It was some time later, while Rose lay draped and soft upon him that Stefan looked up into the blinding flashlight beam. His daughter's shocked voice came from above him. "Daddy!"

"Turn it off, Estelle," he said as quietly as he could manage. When the night was black and safe again, Rose pushed herself from him, and he grunted as her knee hit him again. She hurried to straighten her clothing, bumped her head on the ceiling as she buttoned her shorts, and her elbow hit Stefan's eye as he was sitting up. He rubbed his eye, and to protect Rose at her vulnerable moment, got out of the pickup and faced his daughter. "What are you doing here?"

"What are you? Daddy, did you know this is the local lover's lane? I hope you know about protection and that—"

"Stop. Be quiet." Stefan ran his hands through his hair and stuffed his cotton shirt back into his jeans.

"You could at least take Rose someplace nice, Daddy. Wherever old—I mean, older people go to be alone," Estelle continued in a hushed voice.

Stefan inhaled deeply, wondering why privacy was so difficult to find in Waterville. With Rose in his arms, he had not felt old at all. "I repeat—what are you doing here?"

"Louie came to visit. We were…ah, checking out the local flora and fauna. Grandma is staying with her friends again tonight."

Louie appeared behind her and placed a possessive arm around her shoulders. He smirked at Stefan. "Hi, Pops. You look like you've been steamed, rolled and pressed. Next time you try reverse psychology, like telling me how much work there is here and how much you'd like me to visit, remember that you're dealing with Louie-the-dude."

Before he could stop, Stefan's hand shot out to grasp the front of Louie's shirt. He hauled the youth up close to him. "Listen, you—"

"Daddy…don't you dare!" Estelle cried.

Rose moved from the shadows and stood by Stefan. "Louie, I've heard so much about you," she said in a delighted tone while she pinched Stefan's butt. Stunned, he held very still. The next movement against his bottom was an affectionate pat.

Rose's warning look at him was too deadly to mistake. Stefan released Louie and smiled tightly. After loving Rose, he didn't want an all-out yelling match with his daughter. Donatien tempers, when aroused, weren't sweet. "I'll take Rose home now and see you later."

"You do that, Pops. Rose is hot stuff with all her motors humming, a real biobabe," Louie said with a knowing wink and as Stefan tensed, Rose gave him another warning pinch.

Later, while walking her to her front porch, Stefan finally managed to speak. "I dislike that boy intensely. I do not understand what Estelle sees in him."

"Mmm. Are we having a bad day?" Rose asked in a teasing, cooing tone. "Estelle will handle him." Then, just before she disappeared into her house, she took his face in her hands and pressed tiny kisses all over it. Stefan forgot about Louie and found himself humming as he drove home.

Back home, his head filled with delicious thoughts of Rose, he forced himself to settle Louie comfortably on the downstairs couch; he made certain that Estelle was in her upstairs room. Then he lay down on his bed, still sweetly scented of Rose, and shook his head. *Life used to be uncomplicated. Why wasn't Rose in his arms now, breathing that soft, panting way, her muted cries curling around him?*

When sleep eluded him and he could wait no longer, Stefan knocked lightly on his daughter's bedroom door; he entered after her "I'm awake, Daddy. Come in."

He feared discussing the delicate subject of sex with Estelle; she looked so young and sweet. He paced the room, placing his thoughts in order so that his words would not be so curt. He promised himself he would not say, "I forbid it."

"Daddy, stop thinking so hard," his daughter said quietly. "Don't worry about me having sex with Louie. I think he's disgusting—now since I've had time away from him—now I'm into the clean country boys, with all those muscles and tans and tight buns. And no, I don't have sex. I'm saving myself for the man I really love enough to marry. Louie was just a phase. I've changed so much. I guess it was a rebellion or something, because I'm twenty now and not a silly teenager anymore. Every time you objected to him, I wanted to prove that I could make my own choices, so I kept dating him, even though I knew he is a louse. Rose and I had this discussion a long time ago, and you don't need to worry...but you do need to know about protection. Keep it in your wallet. You never know, and by the way, I think Rose's biological clock has started ticking. She said something about how beautiful you must have been as a little boy. That's stuff a woman says when she's in the mother mode. Wouldn't it be great if it worked out between you and we'd have a big family?"

Stefan stared at her, this girl-woman who was his daughter. Thoughts of babies with Rose danced around his head and he felt himself go all soft and vulnerable inside. "It's been a long day. I'm exhausted," he admitted finally. "And I love you, very, very much. I want only the best for you."

"I know. That's the good part. I know how much you love me, how deeply you care and how hard you've tried to make up for being a single parent. Not every dad would rearrange his work and life, and relocate to make his daughter's dream come true."

His heart filling, Stefan nodded curtly. He rubbed his

eyes, tears burning there. "I think I have a little something in my eyes," he lied. "Sleep tight."

In the shadows of her mother's rose garden, Rose lifted her arms to the moon. Long ago, as a girl, she'd asked the moon to send her faeries for comfort, to hug her and love her as her mother couldn't do.

She dropped her arms and her hands became fists. Why did making love to Stefan open the past? *It had been silent so long, and she had been safe.*

Her father watched her from the back porch and she knew he worried. "He's not like the others, Rose," Maury said gently. "You're going to have to deal with this and what you want. Stefan is a good man, and he hasn't had that many easy times. He's rock-solid. He'll understand, if you tell him. This is something you can't control or shove away. From the looks of things it's time you faced this— you didn't come home last night and Sylvester Frank said that he saw your pickup at the Donatiens' this morning. Come here, and sit by me."

When Rose settled on the steps beside him, Maury took her hand. "I should have been there for you, Rose, but I wasn't. You shouldn't have had to take care of the house— or me and the business, not at such an early age. You went to school some days in the clothes you wore the day before—a pitiful, scraggly little girl with toothpicks for legs."

"We did okay, Dad."

He patted her hand. "You did fine. Not me. I was selfish and the bottle offered me escape from guilt. I knew your mother wanted to travel, but I'd never taken the time to indulge her. I moved in my own world, worked more hours than a happily married man should. Yvette has told me a lot about Stefan and he's succeeded where I failed. He's a man you can trust, Rose. Maybe it's time you thought about making a home of your own, and starting that family. Don't worry about me, I've got plans.''

She looked at him and smiled. ''Want to tell me what they are?''

''Nope, but I can tell you that it's not that easy to find privacy in this town to get to know a woman.''

''Yvette?''

Maury avoided the direct question. ''She's sure opened up my eyes to all the living that is to be done. The thing is, Rose, life moves on. I'll bet that ringing telephone in the house is for you. Better answer it.''

Eight

Stefan's voice coursed low and sexy across the telephone lines. "I'm in our bed."

"Our bed." Rose shivered, though her bedroom wasn't cold. Flashes of the previous night went skimming through her as she settled upon her single bed. She saw Stefan, poised over her, his hair mussed and warm in her fingers, his chest wide and gleaming, his throat taut and a cord pulsing there as he held himself for her greatest pleasure. "I'm sorry about tonight," he said. "I had plans to kiss every beautiful freckle on your body. Why did you come to see me last night?"

Rose was lifting up the neckline of her blouse to see how far her freckles extended downward. "Mmm, what?"

"Why did you come to see me last night? You said you wanted to talk."

She had a few freckles low on her breasts and a dot or two on her stomach, and just a few on her thighs. She remembered how Stefan's big hands had dug in slightly, possessively, and her body started to soften, her hips lifted just slightly— "Hmm? Oh, I wanted to know how it went with Mike and I wanted to give you that check for the roof."

The silence on the other end of the telephone wasn't friendly. "Stefan?" she asked.

"I returned the money as you requested. The matter of the roof isn't up for discussion. I merely wanted to tell you that the morning didn't end as I had planned. I should have brought you breakfast in bed. Crepes, perhaps, with strawberries."

"Stop saying 'bed.'"

After another silence, Stefan murmured, "What's the matter, Rose?"

Her body was humming, aching and Stefan was too far away. "I had a nice time. I meant to tell you so, but I got—mmm—I don't just wake up in bed beside a man every day, you know."

"I know. Perhaps we should do that again sometime. Good night, my darling."

When the line clicked off, Rose held the telephone receiver and stared at it. *"My darling."* Stefan's endearment was her first. She was usually just plain "Rose." She liked being just plain Rose—no fear of being hurt, just one day after another, no more emotional bruises. Rose scooted under her sheets and watched the night wind play with the curtain's lacy ruffles. She couldn't erase Stefan's gentle lovemaking—she'd seen him in action...Stefan would want everything.

She called him back, on the private number he'd given her earlier. "No. Just no. I've tried all this before, and it didn't work. I got all closed-in feeling and sweaty and panicked and we've got to stop right here, Stefan. You saw how I ran out this morning. I didn't mean to, I just did.''

"I thought you said this was a 'share-and-share-alike deal.' That we would make decisions together.''

She recognized that hard, determined voice without the beautiful accent. "You'll be sorry.''

He chuckled. "I don't think so.''

"I'm not dependable in the stretch.''

"I know you are...quite dependable and efficient.''

Rose clenched the telephone. Stefan wasn't backing off. "Are you trying to start an argument, because if you are—''

"You were very soft and tight, my darling. If I hurt you, I'm sorry.''

Rose swallowed, her throat constricting as she remembered how gently Stefan had taken her. "Could we...um, say good-night?''

Stefan began talking softly in French, and though Rose didn't know what he was saying, the rhythm and the deep roll of his voice told her that Stefan was telling her how he wanted to make love to her. When the call ended, Rose lay flat on her bed and shook, her body tensing, remembering every caress the night before, how he had filled her gently.

She swung quickly off the bed and raced for the cold shower. She passed the room her mother had used, now redecorated by Rose. The shadows were still there, the blond woman combing her hair in front of her vanity. Maxine Granger had told her daughter she loved her and then she'd left her.

Rose stepped into the icy water, letting it sluice over her face and tried to forget everything, to wrap herself away from the past—and from Stefan.

* * *

In the morning, Rose flopped over her tangled sheets and turned off her alarm. She just had time for a good, hard run and a nice shower before opening the store. A night of dreaming about Stefan's lovemaking, those soft, sweet kisses, the way he handled her so gently, reverently, didn't allow a deep, restful sleep. At six o'clock in the morning, she stepped out onto her front porch and noted her father coming in the back way, looking very pleased with himself. "Be down to the store later, Rosie," he called. "Need a little shut-eye first and my exercise program for vim and vigor."

She stretched, listened to the birds singing, and jogged down the front steps. She opened the front gate and sailed out onto the street. If she tried hard enough, she could trim away the need to see Stefan, to know if those warm dark eyes really looked at her so intimately.

Just as she sailed around the corner of the street, she noticed Stefan, running toward her. His hair caught the dawn, tousled and gleaming, and his bare chest glistened with sweat. The muscles in his legs bunched and contracted, his stride even, that of an athlete. He looked all warmed up and just right for—Rose's instincts told her to push him down into the lawn behind Mrs. Black's bushes and have him.

But that wouldn't do. She'd get used to having him on a regular basis and the next thing she knew, it would be the end of summer and she'd be looking at heartbreak trail. She turned, heading the other direction, and picked up speed. He quickly closed the distance. "Louie is gone. Estelle took him for a walk last night in the pasture. He stepped in a fresh cowpile. Then later, at the lake, he experienced his first authentic chiggers, which seemed to have caused him discomfort during the night. It appears that my mother and daughter forgot to tell him of the dangers of walking through brush without insect repellent," Stefan said, running easily beside her. "My mother came in too happy this morning. Do you know anything about that?"

Rose kept running. She had an idea why Yvette's happiness might match Maury's smile. "No. But this is my street. Not yours. I run here every morning. Well, except for yesterday."

Running beside her, their strides matching, Stefan was…delectable. They ran side by side beneath the shady oak trees, with the dawn skipping through the leaves and the mockingbirds singing, just as they did every morning. For a while, the paper boy pedaled his bicycle beside them and chatted with Stefan about prime fishing worms called "nightcrawlers" and where to dig for them.

When they were alone—the boy riding ahead and sailing his papers onto front porches or on top of shrubs—Stefan shot Rose one of those intimate, dark glances that ripped down her body, heating it more. "You have sweat between your breasts. They are bobbing gently and I remember the taste of them, the shape in my hand, how readily your body opens to mine," he stated unevenly. "I would like to kiss you, just there, where the sweat makes your shirt cling to you. How long do you think you can keep your secrets, Rose?"

"What secrets?" A wave of panic slammed into her. Stefan was definitely too close for comfort.

Stefan reached for her arm and slowed her to a stop. He wrapped his arms around her and drew her close, studying her as they tried to catch their breaths. "When you tell me, I'll know that you trust me. Trust is important for you and for me. But you are my lover and I am yours and you have my heart. I do not give it lightly, but I cherish you as you are, a delight and a beautiful, loving, exciting woman. You can call me, if you wish—at night, when you think of me.''

''I've never done that in my life, Stefan. I can't imagine talking to a man like that.''

''And I've never spoken so to a woman. But isn't it a wonderful time to start, just after making love?'' With that, he tugged her closer and gave her a kiss that tore through her like wildfire.

Stefan reached low to cup her bottom and lift her against him, her arms encircling him. ''I could pin you in two seconds flat,'' she whispered, when she could speak. She pulled his damp hair back, easing his face up to hers, and looked down at him. ''If I wanted to.''

''You want to seduce me. I see it in your lovely sky-blue eyes. I see it in your freckles. They want to attack me. To rub themselves all over my naked body until I melt into a mindless pool of gelatin.''

''That's not possible,'' Rose whispered raggedly because Stefan was already hard against her.

Stefan lowered her to the ground and his hungry look at her breasts started them peaking. Then he smiled tightly, turned and set off jogging on the road toward his house.

When Rose stared after him, thinking how nice and tight his backside was, Mrs. Wilkins called, ''You'll have to run faster than that, Rose. He's a mover. And he's the kind that will want to marry you. Not just waltz up to the altar and bolt. Sonny is out for the whole tamale. That's why he's taking his time.''

By the first of August, Rose was having difficulty concentrating on paint and wallpaper samples, and on ordering fall carpet samples. Business was slow, though she expected the usual fall rush—when Estelle went to college and the Donatiens packed up and left Waterville. Maury was looking better every day, losing weight, his color returning. He began puttering around the house and would often go home in the middle of the day to fix the plumbing. He usually returned near to closing time with quite a cheery look. Rose could only hope that Maury would enjoy his life as much when the Donatiens left. He would miss— Rose didn't want to think about what Maury might miss with Yvette, other than her friendship. "Don't worry about me," he'd told her frequently when she worried. "I've got plans."

With his help, Rose had more time to run in the morning and Stefan usually met her. It was comfortable with him, running through the dawn, forgetting everything and settling into the routine. She liked routines; they were safe.

She loved to sit with him at sunset. Stefan's childhood hadn't been wild and free like her own; he'd led a structured life, pushed by a demanding father, and made bearable by a loving mother. Stefan seemed to enjoy listening to stories of young Rose's escapades, such as rescuing kittens from the tops of trees. When she described going into a narrow cave to rescue puppies, he became very quiet. "Where were your parents?"

She had shaken her head. They'd both been occupied— her mother with her lover and her father with his broken heart.

Stefan's evening calls were not routine in Rose Granger's life, because whatever he was saying in French, so dark and sweet, caused her to tremble and tighten and dream of him. Their lovemaking seemed too delicious to be real now, because Stefan appeared to have withdrawn slightly, which was what Rose usually expected of the men who were briefly interested in her. He seemed less interested about wanting her. When they had met, he felt like more of a companion, a bud, a friend, than the man who called her every night and turned her to one big, molten shivering ache.

Well, then, Rose thought as their paths met or they jogged together and Stefan bent to kiss her cheek, or touch her hair. His expression was warm and tender, when she really wanted that sexy, smoldering sensual look. *She had another bud, when she wanted a lover.*

And then, the whole town was gossiping about Maggie White and how she seemed to be purring and content— her usual when she was being satisfied on a regular basis.

Rose looked out of the store's windows and sighted Stefan's truck at Danny's Café. She'd worried enough about Stefan rolling in Maggie's experienced arms, a known man-zapper. After a full fifteen minutes of walking back and forth in the store and trying to concentrate on an attractive display of brushes, Rose had had enough. It was only two o'clock in the afternoon and her father would be back soon. She flipped over the Open sign to Closed and locked the door as she crossed the street to the café. If Stefan was enjoying Maggie's charms, Rose wanted to know.

When she entered, she saw Stefan back in the kitchen; Danny's bulk was threatening a bar stool. He was discussing summer heat and slow business with the spit and whittle bench-men, who had moved inside Danny's to take advantage of the air conditioning. Rose nodded to Danny and the elderly men and walked back into the kitchen, taking in Stefan's chest-to-thigh cook's apron over his white T-shirt and jeans. Despite her dark mood, it struck her how comfortable the scene was—Danny taking a break and Stefan cooking.

He looked nothing like the stiletto-lean man in his Chicago office; he looked nothing like the lover who had betrayed her with Maggie White.

He smiled briefly at her and then gave his attention to braising the slices of a large pot roast and placing them in a Dutch oven. "Beef *Arlesienne,*" he explained and with a flourish, added fresh, peeled country tomatoes, mushrooms and olives. If she hadn't been worried about Maggie zapping Stefan, Rose might have enjoyed the artistry of his movements, the little experienced flourishes. She wanted his full concentration when she asked him the vital question and decided to wait. Stefan deftly smashed garlic cloves with the flat of a chef's knife and tossed them into the mixture. Fresh, chopped basil was next, followed by bay leaves, and then Stefan covered the heavy pot and placed it on the back of the big cookstove. "There," he said, as he washed his hands in the big kitchen sink. "Now I can talk. Danny wanted something different for tonight. He doesn't feel like cooking, so I made a little coq au vin—chicken with wine—a little braised cabbage, a little dressing for his usual salad, and he will provide the required mashed potatoes."

He studied her. "You look hot. Let me get you a glass of ice water."

While he went to the fountain area in the front of the café, Rose tapped her toe and thought of how she would ask him about Maggie. When he admitted seeing Maggie, Rose would be calm, unaffected and simply go back to her life without him.

Stefan returned and handed her the large glass of ice water—which Rose promptly threw at him. Water hissed and beaded on the large grill and Stefan shook the droplets from his face, then wiped his hand across it. "And what, may I ask, is the problem?"

"Maggie. You've been seeing her." She'd never been jealous and hated the fiery cords running through her now.

Stefan frowned, then slowly took the mop and wiped up the floor. "And you don't like it?" he asked thoughtfully.

"You can't just call me every night and say whatever you're saying, and run with me every morning, and then— there was that time about two weeks ago—and then *take up with Maggie.*"

"You want me? Alone? For yourself? Why?" Stefan asked very carefully, as he studied her. A drop of water fell from the shelf over the grill and sizzled on it, mimicking Rose's temper. She did not have a nasty temper, and yet, here it was.

Rose threw up her hands. "Hey, I don't have a problem. No, I don't want you. Not me, no way. Stop rapping questions at me."

Stefan began to smile slowly and then he wrapped his arms around her and walked back into the storeroom, closing them in the darkness with the canned goods. He pulled on a cord and the bald light trapped her. She wanted to shield her expression, to prevent Stefan from seeing how angry and hurt she was, but instead she glared at him, her emotions too stormy for her to speak.

Stefan studied her closely, tugged the cord again and the room was dark and scented of him. He pulled her into his arms, not tenderly, but with just the edge of possession, and his mouth fused to hers. Not gently, or persuasively, but with the stamp of a man who desired her without caution. She heard a click and knew her control had snapped.

The wild, sweet taste shot through her like a rocket and she locked her arms around him, meeting that desire with her own. His hands were on her breasts, shaping them, tormenting her gently, and then her bra came free and his mouth scorched her skin, his suckling tearing away all the frustration she'd had every night and day. She ran her hands under his shirt and he quickly stripped it away, pulling her tightly against him, his mouth hot and open on hers.

"Stefan. Now," she whispered raggedly as he unsnapped her shorts, they fell to her ankles, and his caresses began that fiery journey. Riveted there, held by her own desire for him, Rose cried out, holding him tightly. His voice rushed to curl around her, driving her pleasure higher as she dug her fingers into his hair, locking his lips to hers, taking and giving. Then the rush of pleasure shot over her and she sagged with the force, her knees unable to hold her. His kisses slowed and sweetened and soothed. "*Chérie*, for me, there is no other woman. I live for the taste of you, the feel of you."

"Mmm," she managed to say when a "Likewise" was churning in her mind.

Stefan rocked her gently against him until she managed to catch her breath. "Better now?" he asked gently as she felt his smile curling against her temple.

She could only nod and meet the sweet, tender, searching, reassuring kiss he gave her. "I cannot leave now. There are the last-minute sauces...the eggplant meunière. Sit and talk with me," he asked, his hands caressing. "It's good to talk with you. It gives me ease. Your voice is like music, but your body—"

Stefan's telling muscles tightened and quivered around her and his hands swept downward to cup her bottom, drawing her tightly against him.

That was all the reassurance she needed to know that Stefan had not adjourned with Maggie. Rose reached to smooth his hair; she stood on tiptoe and kissed him because he deserved kissing and tenderness. Their kisses were brief and meaningful, giving her a peace she hadn't known.

Because Danny's "French Night" was crowded, Rose

stayed to help Suzie serve the people. Danny and Stefan made an odd pair and everyone barely noticed the yelling in the kitchen. First Danny quit, surging his bulk out of the kitchen, and tearing off his apron and sitting to glower at the remaining contender. Then regrouping, he put on his apron again and pushed his bulk back into the kitchen. Stefan was next, stalking out of the kitchen, muttering darkly in French, and tearing off his apron. He stood, seemingly transfixed as Rose looked at him. Then he walked to her and asked her, "If I get through this night, I will be nothing but shreds of my former self. You know that, don't you?"

Rose may not have been experienced in lovemaking, or handling a too-interested male, but she did understand how to make peace. She wanted Stefan to fit into the difficult situation, while Danny wasn't ready to admit the newcomer in the cooking ring. Timing was everything; if this conflict weren't resolved now, Stefan would lose kitchen rights and possibly his temper, and Danny's would be off limits. "I know. But you're always so wonderful in difficult situations. You run Donatien's Restaurants, an entire chain. I've seen you in action. You know exactly when to be firm and when to relent."

Stefan considered that thought. "Yes, I do, don't I?"

"Danny has always been a little touchy about his weight." She wanted Stefan to avoid that pitfall.

"It is difficult to fit into that small space with him," Stefan muttered. "But I have not said anything."

"Of course you wouldn't, because you're considerate of other people. Think of how you're helping him and think of how difficult it would be for you to give up the helm of Donatien's. Give Danny time to think about all the wonderful things you're doing for him. He just needs time to adjust. Just compliment him on his dishes and he'll be more acceptable of yours. He loves to cook, so you share a common interest, if not the exact recipes. And he is very, very careful about food preparation. Every vegetable is washed thoroughly, and his kitchen has always been very clean. In that, he's just like you, very neat and clean. You're like generals in the same army, but with individual styles that work well together. You'll see.''

Stefan scowled at the kitchen, clearly considering Rose's thoughts. ''Yes, perhaps that is true. He is very good about washing vegetables and cleanliness. Not every chef—cook—is so cautious and I admire his slicing and dicing techniques... I merely added a little wine to his tasteless chicken and he exploded.''

''Think of Danny's dishes as ethnic food—Italian, French or soul. But instead it's good old Missourian. It has a right to distinct flavor and presentation, too. The point is, people around here like it. You're wonderful at give-and-take relationships. Look how you're coping with your life here. Your family worked together to redo that old house. Danny really likes you, you know.'' She patted his cheek with her free hand while balancing Mr. Peterson's berry pie with the other.

Leroy Evans popped in and asked if Stefan was cooking tonight. When Stefan frowned at him, Leroy quickly exited the café. Rose wondered about his boyish grin, because Leroy, a dairy farmer usually kept to himself. His wife had passed away years ago, and the usually solemn man quietly tended his land.

In Stefan's frustration, his hands running through his hair and that dark scowl on his face, he looked hot and sweet and delicious, just perfect for—but then she remembered that Stefan had pleasured her and asked nothing in return. She didn't want to be the cause of him losing the

kitchen battle. "You're not going to give up, are you?"
she asked sweetly. "Not when there are people to be fed?"

"You think I would give up? *Me, Stefan Donatien, master chef, give up?*" With a grim expression, Stefan
whipped on his apron and returned to the kitchen. After a
few more moments of the two men arguing loudly, they
settled into a low rumble. Later, after the crowd cleared,
Danny and Stefan sat in a booth, discussing the fresh farm
vegetables and "Italian Night." Stefan reached to tug Rose
down by his side, holding her hand. It all seemed very
natural and good and safe, Rose thought, looking at Stefan's big hand laced with hers. *But summer was ending....*

Summer was ending too soon, Stefan thought as he sat
in his home office, the second week of August. In another
three weeks, Estelle would be away at school, and her
giggling and racing through the house to meet friends
would stop. Stefan frowned slightly—he still hadn't con-
vinced Estelle to bring her friends home for dinner and a
movie, which was a test he just couldn't pass as a rural
parent.

At night, he'd finished studying the figures that his Donatien's Restaurant account firm had given him. Business
was good, but there was another problem, according to his
manager—a known restaurant pest was circling each one
of the restaurants. This woman and her husband were
known for suing—falling on flooring that wasn't slick,
finding insects in food that they planted there, feigning
sickness from food.

Stefan tossed his pen to the table and listened to the
window air conditioner hum. He knew that there would
always be a business problem that would require his personal attention—grand openings, celebrity dinners, promotional events that marked Donatien's presence in the

Chicago restaurant scene. The expansion plan he'd put into effect the previous year was requiring decisions and meetings, and his top man was going through a divorce—his torn emotions were affecting his work. His errors would take time and patience to unravel and they were costly.

Stefan's father would have never allowed Tim Place to continue working after his first error, let alone his others. But Stefan thought the investment in Tim, letting him take time to resolve his life, was a good one. The Donatiens had always made the important decisions and Stefan would eventually have to go back to the city. He was determined to see the summer through, until Estelle returned to college. An absence from Rose would diminish any delicate relationship they had established. He would not push and she would not surrender—

Rose still didn't trust him. He could taste it in her good-night kisses—the desire and the reluctance to fully trust him. He ran with her every morning, watched her determination to withhold herself from him, never giving over freely. They walked and talked and ate ice-cream cones, but Rose seemed to be drawing away from him. *She was sealing herself from him, protecting herself against pain.*

While they ran, a greyhound named Walt sometimes joined them. They slowed their pace for the old dog, and Rose explained how Walt sometimes slept on her front porch when his master was in the hospital. In winter, she kept him in the warm back porch. But she couldn't bear to take Walt, when his master passed away, and so he had become everyone's pet, and loved by all. That example told Stefan how carefully she guarded her heart.

She ran gently through the lives in Waterville, resolving differences just as she had with Stefan's Danny incident. But Rose never came too close to love's commitment.

His fatigue was telling, and he thought it wisest not to

bother Rose with his problems. She would only interpret that to mean he would be leaving her life and returning to business. Stefan ran his hand over his jaw, the sound of stubble there scraping in the quiet room. He was tired, and one glance in the mirror told him of the shadows his face wore, the lines more distinct. Balancing a large scale, fast-paced business from a distance wasn't easy, and he'd been too abrupt with the office manager.

He wasn't pushing Rose, Stefan promised himself, though every instinct he possessed told him to claim her. More than once, after an evening walk, they had kissed and Rose had ignited, the sounds coming low and deep inside of her triggering his own desire. He would not push her to give him something so precious as her trust; yet it wounded him that her shadows were stronger than the love they could have. Rose needed to make her own decisions and the tension ran through them like the hot, muggy air after a summer rain.

The humming tension in his body nudged Stefan. There was no escaping the fact that they should be making love each night and weren't.

Rose had protected herself all of her life and she wasn't committing to a relationship she feared might hurt her. If he told her of his love, and the marriage he wanted, he could frighten her badly.

Rose needed time to adjust to the change in her life. And time was running short for Stefan. He eventually would have to return to Chicago, and the gap between Rose and him might widen, because Rose had said many times that Waterville was her life. He couldn't imagine plucking her from it. He couldn't imagine her being happy anywhere else. *What kind of a marriage could he offer her—flying back and forth on business, the late nights and the dilemmas? Rose deserved those children she had wanted, and they deserved a full-time father…if Estelle were right and Rose's biological clock was ticking, Stefan preferred that he be the father of her children.*

He smiled at the thought of blue-eyed, freckle-faced girls in braids—long-legged, beguiling faerie imps, climbing up trees to rescue kittens and taking time to ease wounded hearts.

Stefan listened to the creak of his mother's bedroom, her footsteps down the hallway and onto the stairs. Soon the back door opened and closed and he knew she would not return until morning.

A fax listing the new employee benefits package purred out of the machine. He firmed his lips, disliking the idea that his mother would meet a man in secret. And no righteous man would make her do so—Maury needed to have his daughter's inner strength.

Rose was very close to her father. If Stefan accused Maury of being less than honorable, he would have to deal with Rose. Stefan shook his head and then he called Larry and Henry. Much as he resented asking for Rose's ex-fiancés' help, he would need them in the next few days.

Nine

Rose listened carefully to Estelle's hushed whisper over the telephone. "It's Daddy. I told him that my friends were coming over for a little party. We've only got a week until September comes and everyone takes off to their different colleges. We were just going to watch movies and have some hot dogs and potato chips and sit around and talk. *You've got to come.* Daddy is all set to cook a full meal and he'll be hurt if we don't eat it. But the kids won't like tournedos with cream, and crepes for dessert. Jason is a botany major. He's bound to say that mushrooms are spores, and he won't eat them. There isn't anything else they'd like, and if we leave, he'll really be hurt. *You've got to come. You always know the right thing to say and do,*" she repeated desperately.

Rose frowned slightly as she replaced the telephone. Stefan had seemed distracted for the past week, and shadows brewed beneath his eyes. He seemed to be a man caught in a dilemma, and he wasn't sharing it with her. People usually shared their problems with Rose, and she didn't like being unable to help Stefan when he needed her. At times, while they were walking, she sensed he was about to say something serious, and then he shifted the conversation to the ordinary. Stefan was always a man in control—what could worry him so?

The answer came back—business. Stefan was leaving and he was debating how to tell her. She had to make certain that he knew one night of loving was not a commitment for life, though she would hold it dear forever.

He'd called at night, that deep, husky voice coursing over the lines in beautiful language she didn't understand. But in the distance, another telephone rang and faxes whirred, and Stefan's curse came short and dark. He'd apologized, but she sensed his great strain and impatience.

She sniffed delicately, trying to minimize the slight bruise. She had handled her problems and most of the town's for years and she was a known "soft heart."

At eight o'clock in the evening, Eb's Grocery had closed for his birthday. Rose dialed Danny and a half hour later, she pulled into the Donatiens' driveway. Estelle rushed out to meet her and Rose handed her boxes of buns and chips from the back of her pickup. When Rose turned to lift the box of hamburger patties and wieners, Stefan loomed over her. "Oh, hi, Stefan."

"I will cook these," he said very formally. "*This* is why I trained in France," he muttered darkly. "To be a fry cook in my own home. No, wait. I've graduated to the barbecue grill."

Estelle's eyes widened at his sarcasm as Rose gave her the bucket container of potato salad. "Daddy—"

Yvette took the sack of lettuce, tomatoes and pickles.

"He is in a bad mood. At times he is like his father, too stiff to bend."

Stefan seemed to growl at her. "Was I wrong to want to know the name of the man you are seeing? Am I not your son? Do I not have that right?"

The clash between son and mother was easy to see, and Rose ached for both of them as Yvette's accent deepened. "I am tired of men's rights. I have my own as a woman who has lived and loved, and wants to love even more."

In an uncustomary show of anger, Yvette glared at him. "You are up all night, calling and faxing and punching your money keys. You will work yourself into an early grave, just like him. Always the restaurant business when life waited. It was Guy's dream and his fear of failure. His life. You should have your own dreams and your own life. When you return to Chicago, you will once again slide into that cold grave your father prepared you for. Oh, I fought, but I lost. Failure does not only apply to business, it applies to life. Take life, Stefan, embrace and enjoy it. Rose has been good for you, and we are all much better for her in our lives— Tend to your own romance, Stefan, and do not make the mistakes that your father did. If he had said, 'I forbid' one more time—"

With that, she walked back into the house, and with a worried, helpless look, Estelle followed her.

Clearly at odds with the women in his family, Stefan looked frustrated and nettled. "I have the grill ready," he said, in a doomed tone. "For hamburgers and hot dogs."

Because he looked so disturbed, slapping the hamburger patties onto the grill and standing with his spatula like a spear at the ready, Rose wanted to ease him. She placed the flat of her hand on his back, felt that powerful ripple of tension. "I love tournedos with cream," she said in her best I'm-really-starved voice.

She wasn't certain exactly what Stefan's dish was, but she wanted to help as the hamburgers sizzled on the grill. Yvette set the picnic table, clearly ignoring Stefan, before returning to the house. "She has a lover," Stefan brooded. "They are all growing up and leaving me. No one needs me."

Rose didn't know what to do except to lean against Stefan's back. He seemed so alone and brooding and she wanted to help. She knew the comfort in being needed. "I do. I need you. I haven't eaten tonight and I'm dying for your tournedos."

His "Hmm" sounded disbelieving. She placed her cheek against his back, smoothing the strength of it. She realized how much she liked holding him, comforting him and sharing. The hours were flying by now, when Estelle would go to college, and Stefan would eventually return to his business. "Are you back in control now?"

"No, stay there. It is the only good thing that has happened all day—your breasts against my back, your hands on me."

Yvette walked to them and smiled tightly at Rose. Clearly her anger at Stefan was still brewing. "I have not finished. He thinks Maury and I are having an affair. That is not so. Maury and Leroy and Maggie White and I were going to double date tonight, but since Stefan is no fit company to chaperon, I invited them over to show these young people how to swing dance."

"My father? Dancing?" Rose asked and rummaged through her memory. Not a trace of Maury's dancing appeared. *But Maggie White was an excellent swing dancer.*

Yvette faced Stefan, a woman determined to make her point. "I think I will marry Leroy, Stefan. He loves cows and good cheese as much as I do, and we have much in common. I have been lonely for years, despite my social life, and it is time I had a man in my bed. You see, passion is not only for the young, and Leroy seems to be getting more so all the time. He is a gentle man, if not the first love of my life. If you have objections, they will wait until we are alone.''

''Maggie White,'' Rose murmured and walked to sit on the picnic bench. She rubbed the ache in her temple. It all made sense now. No wonder her father was trying so desperately to get in better shape. No wonder he needed rest. No wonder he took lengthy noon breaks. No wonder Maggie had been so friendly lately. ''I always thought I'd lose him to poor health, not to a woman,'' she said as the summer night swirled around her.

''Rose...'' Stefan's tone was concerned.

''Huh? I don't want to be here when Maggie and Dad arrive. When he's ready, he'll tell me. I'm going home.''

Stefan ran his hand through his hair, studying her closely as if he feared for her. ''You haven't eaten.''

Then because he looked just as uncertain as she, Rose said, ''Bring carry-in. Those tournedos things.''

Rose hurried to find that special dress in the back of her closet. Stefan had looked so stricken at his mother's announcement, and nettled by his daughter's food preferences, that Rose wanted to dress especially for his tournedos with cream or whatever else he wanted to cook. Cooking provided Stefan with a release, she'd discovered, and while he would be polite to his guests, he would be brooding about his empty nest.

She was used to empty nests, and when her father told her of Maggie, she would be prepared to be happy for him, if not for herself. Was it so selfish to want to keep him with her? To know that he was always there—snoring and safe—in the next room?

What kind of a woman was she anyway, to want to keep her father from love? Just because she'd had heartbreak as a child, didn't mean that others should give up their lives for her. Rose blinked, shocked by the idea flashing in her mind—maybe Maury had drives she hadn't thought of—maybe he had needed alcohol to get a reprieve. After that night of lovemaking with Stefan, Rose better understood the result of denying the body's and the heart's needs.

Rose eased herself into the dress then shivered delicately as she stared at her freckles rising on her breasts in their too-tight confinement. She could almost feel his mouth against her—a tingling shot down to her lower body as she remembered his lovemaking.

Rose closed her eyes, remembering what Stefan had said—he'd only made love to his wife and then no one else until Rose. He wasn't a man to take lovemaking lightly, rather he gave it the same intensity as he did everything else. Stefan was not a hit-and-miss guy; once started on a course, he usually followed it until the end.

The preparation and serving of food would soothe Stefan and she would share how she felt, and she would listen, and perhaps he wouldn't feel so alone.

Rose frowned. Alone was not a good feeling. She didn't want Stefan to feel alone. She wanted to give him something, and because she was just a bit selfish—she wanted to take something, too. She added a little shade of smoke to her lids, to darken her eyes. A little lip gloss and a few pins to lift her hair off her shoulders in an attempt at sophistication, and she was ready for Stefan's dinner. She studied the tight black dress, which emphasized her long legs. She turned, viewing her backside in the mirror, then inhaled whatever courage she could rummage. Stefan came from a sophisticated world, and she didn't even have perfume to go with the outfit. Rose thought about cooking vanilla and dismissed the idea—Stefan would recognize the sweet scent immediately.

She turned to face the mirror. "This is it—all I've got for a fancy dinner. Just a plain old dress that I've really grown out of, and some Christmas candles on the table. So much for giving Stefan something else to think about."

Maybe it was wrong, but she was just selfish enough to want one more night in Stefan's arms. She wanted to hoard the taste of him, the feel of his body against hers, that rush of his breath across her cheek.

She heard the doorbell and smiled briefly—Stefan was always so proper. She looked in the mirror once more, noting the flush on her cheeks, the excitement dancing around her. She almost felt sorry for Stefan, because he was coming for consolation and dinner and she intended to zap him. They'd grown to be friends, running together each day, and walking together in the evening. He would be unsuspecting....

She tossed away her guilt on the way downstairs. Summer was coming to an end and Stefan would be gone soon. She cared for him, trusted him with her body, and he had not disappointed her with his gentleness. A woman had few chances in life to experience a man like Stefan before she settled down again into the comfort of spinsterhood and godmothering. Rose smoothed her dress and breathed deeply and opened the door to Stefan.

His gaze ran down her body, touching on the bodice that was too tight and pushed her breasts upward. His eyes darkened as he studied the tight fit covering her hips and the hem that just barely touched her midthighs. When he placed the basket on the floor, just inside the door, she thought she'd lost him. Then his darkened gaze ran back up her body to her lips, which she moistened because she was terribly nervous. He didn't speak, but his body tensed—she could feel the impact upon hers as Stefan stood, considering every feature of her face and those slow looks down her body caused her to shake.

"The dress is old, but I thought it might suit your fancy dinner." Rose Granger didn't like uncertainty, and now she knew that she'd lost trying to seduce the man who had become her "bud." In fishing terms, she'd just lost the nibble. The bait wasn't right; the hook wasn't set.

"The dress is fine. I like it very much. I like the way the light dances over the freckles on your breasts. They are creamy and soft and quivery every time you breathe.... Take it off," Stefan said huskily as he stepped inside her house and closed the door behind him.

Rose had just time to blink in disbelief and then Stefan's arms were around her, his mouth on hers and that wild, sweet hunger shot through her like a lightning bolt. His hand tugged down the zipper, flattened to her back and searched. "No bra," he whispered unevenly as if he had discovered the ultimate delight. He seemed to vibrate, held still by the thought before diving into the kiss.

She was certain a volcano had struck Waterville; she could almost feel the ground rumbling, if Stefan hadn't lifted her off her feet. The dress slid from her and she arched into the kisses that ran from her lips to her throat and downward. Stefan was hot and hard and shaking against her, and she needed him to be complete, the ache growing almost painfully.

"Rose," he whispered roughly, swinging her up into his arms. Once again, he carried her upstairs, to the small feminine room that was hers. But Rose stopped him, nodding to another room. There in the shadows, with the window air conditioner humming and the world shut outside, Rose watched Stefan's tight expression as he lowered her to the double bed and quickly stripped off his clothes. The dim light outlined his tall body, those shoulders, that tapering waist and narrow hips and long, powerful legs. Just the sight of him eased Rose's tension, because she knew he wanted her as desperately as she wanted him. That knowledge wiped away any idea that she wasn't appealing, or feminine and nestled within her like a warm, sweet flower bud. She reached out to touch him, needing no gentle time between them, only the doing, and the pleasure.

When he came down on her gently, his body shook, and all the heat and lightning of a summer storm enclosed her. The bed was old and creaked with his weight as he braced himself over her. He smoothed her hair over the pillow, kissed the slender hand that tenderly stroked his warm cheek, comforting even as she aroused.

Stefan's hand slid down the sweep and dip and softness of the woman he loved. Just there was her soft hip—he dug his fingers in slightly, possessively, wildfire raging within him. Her thighs were smooth and quivering, desire dancing between them. He tensed as she found his nipple, gently biting it, and then Stefan touched her intimately, and the jolt flattened her to the sheets. He whispered to her quickly now, the rush of sweet, dark words careening around her, sweeping up inside, heated by his lips on her body.

She opened to him, the blunt pressure filling her, completing her, Stefan holding her so closely they were one. The storm came quickly, flashing and pulsing and still he wanted more, and she gave more, gathering him close to her, stroking his back, nipping his shoulder as the world whirled and caught fire and blazed, her muscles straining for release that seemed so close.

Stefan's body flowed with hers, familiar and bold and hungry. His lips and tongue battled gently with hers for she would have the taste of him, the desire that sparkled and tormented and pleased. His hands ran over her, caressing, cupping, touching. She dug her fingertips into his upper arms, caught the power there and took it into her, hoarding it. Within the pounding rhythm came a bloodred heat and she clung to Stefan, matching him until the world quivered and stood still and released its warm flood.

She rested her cheek on his chest as he came to lie close and snug against her, their passion still joined as each was reluctant to leave what had passed. She stroked his taut body, his heartbeat slowing its race, and enjoyed the soothing of him, this man she had taken. He kissed her forehead and smoothed back her hair. "I missed you."

Rose moved to lie over him, her lover, pinning him to the bed. She looked down into his face, those blunt cheekbones, those dark brown eyes, and traced a thick eyebrow. "I missed you," she returned, praying that he wouldn't leave her too soon.

The admission startled her, for she was not one to give it lightly, intimately. Stefan smoothed her cheek, studying her. "It's not good away from you, Rose," he said too quietly.

"I know." She waited for the panic that came when people got too close and it didn't come. She knew how much she missed him, how she dreamed of him holding her warm and safe. This time their kisses were more gentle, the first fiery hunger fed. Slowly, carefully, their lips fitted and brushed and lifted and Stefan's caresses treasured her breasts, her back, her bottom. He stroked her intimately then, and the motion became a soft desire and then Stefan's body completed them as they rocked gently, savoring the intimacy, the pleasure, the completion. In the creaking of the old bed, she found comfort and safety. In Stefan, she found answers that both frightened and pleased her.

Later, she lay quietly in his arms, listening to the old

house settle. The branches of the old oak tree scraped gently against the rain gutter she needed to clean. But all she wanted to do now was rest in Stefan's arms. She realized that peace wasn't a commodity she'd experienced very much in her life; she'd had to battle too hard to keep her walls up.

"This isn't your room," Stefan noted softly as the shadows quivered around them.

"No. It's hers. I redid it years ago. I scrubbed away everything that was hers and still she stayed in me. If she would have lived until I was grown up, I'd have told her how awful she was—to tell a child she loved her and then to run away on a cheap thrill and never come back. I spent hours up in that tree, watching the road for the first sight of her coming home. Before I gave up hope of becoming a mother, I feared how awful I would be, and would I have enough love for a child. And then after telling me she loved me she would tell me the truth—that I was unwanted and an 'accident' that trapped her. Would I want to abandon my own child?" Rose wished the bitterness weren't there, but it was. She'd released it to no one else, but Stefan.

"You would love your child," Stefan said firmly and his hand flattened low on her stomach. He caressed it gently, thoughtfully. "And I do not think that you should completely give up that idea. You would make a wonderful mother."

She struggled against the tears that burned her lids and slid, one by one, onto Stefan's bare chest. "It's silly, I know. I never cry. Never. I haven't told anyone else, and now I have someone else to remember in this room."

She lifted suddenly, feeling very vulnerable and feminine. "Stefan, I planned to seduce you tonight. You just wouldn't fit into my bed, so—"

"I am honored. I very much enjoyed the pleasure and it's a lovely room. Thank you for sharing it with me."

"I'm not done with you yet." She looked down to where Stefan had placed his mouth—on the tender skin between her thumb and her index finger. He gently nibbled and sucked and she realized she couldn't breathe. Sensations were already purring and revved, simmering and hungry. "That's nice. Keep it up."

"Oh, I intend to."

Later, Stefan spread his reheated dinner on the kitchen table. He mourned the sauce's texture and lit the Christmas candles. He wanted a life with Rose, a wedding and a family. He would have to move very carefully so as not to frighten her while she dealt with her ghosts. He knew that she had shared more with him than with anyone else, and that they were cruising into trouble—abstaining for a takeover had been difficult and he'd almost asked her to marry him. He would have to make the right decision for Rose and for his family. Yvette and Estelle and he had worked together as a team on the old house and were growing closer every day. But he needed Rose. Was it asking too much to marry the woman he loved? *He wanted to wake up every morning in their marriage bed.*

The telephone rang, and Rose answered. She frowned slightly as if puzzled. "Yes, that's Stefan's pickup outside. You want to speak with him? Henry has plans for tonight? What do you mean, Henry has plans?"

Stefan hurried to take the telephone from her. He spoke in a hushed, firm tone, similar to those in spy movies. "Not tonight. I will contact you."

Rose studied him as he disconnected the line. Stefan had sounded very determined. "What's up?"

"I'm trying to bond with your ex-fiancés. We're having an all-men's night soon. I apologize, but I will be unavailable to you at that time," Stefan said very carefully as he admired the long, curved line of her body beneath his T-shirt. It all seemed too good to be true, cooking in a home kitchen, wearing his boxer shorts while his love hungrily eyed dinner.

"Henry and Larry used to invite me along for those late-night fishing trips. When we were younger, I had to dig and provide worms. They're older, and they left me alone in a cemetery while we were snipe hunting. Dad made them apologize and explain to me that there weren't any such creatures—you're getting ready to leave Waterville, aren't you? You're bored and ready to get back into the swing of things. That's what your mother was talking about, wasn't it? That you miss the city and the action?"

Stefan turned to face her. He placed aside the plate he had just filled. He concentrated on finding the right words and not frightening Rose. "Surely you know that I have found enough 'action' here, with you."

"I can't imagine you staying here permanently." Rose's bald statement hit the room. She gripped the back of a chair for an anchor. She would miss him all her life, but she'd had this unique time to remember and cherish.

"My mother is happy here, so is my daughter. They are already planning holidays. There is no reason I could not be happy here, too. I am considering making arrangements to remain here—with you."

The kitchen was suddenly too quiet and tense, waves of emotion hitting Rose. "I've seen you in a business meeting. You're tough and there's an excitement dancing around you, like a warrior going into battle. Estelle and Yvette may stay, but you need that edge, that challenge. It's as if you're pitting yourself against all odds and enjoying it. There's nothing to fight in Waterville, Stefan. If you came back at times—that's visiting, not living day-today, watching the gardens and the children grow and the elderly age.''

''True, and those are good battles, ones to fill the heart. Do you think so little of me, that I have no heart?''

She couldn't bear to hurt Stefan's feelings and returned quickly, ''You've got a marvelous, generous, loving heart. Look what you've done—no easy matter to take time away from your company to live here. But that other part of you needs something else.''

''Yes, it does need something else—you.''

Rose placed her hand on her throat, which had just tightened as she panicked. ''Did you think, my darling,'' Stefan said too softly, with an edge of temper brewing in his words, ''that I would want your body and not your heart?''

''That last faerie is a little slanted, old buddy. If her tutu tips any more, I'll see up her skirt,'' Larry noted as he sipped his beer, then placed the bottle on the sundial held by a faerie statue. ''Better prop that wooden one up straight before it falls on that fern.''

Henry held up his beer and used it to sight the upright faerie, with wings glistening in the September 1 moonlight. The leaves rattled gently overhead, the oaks preparing for fiery autumn color. The roses in the Granger garden were still lush and huge, but soon they would fall on the faeries that now stood in various poses in the garden. The largest ones were concrete and gleamed in the moonlight; the more delicately fashioned polyresins seemed lighter, their gauzelike clothing almost floating in the slight breeze. The artist had given the wings special care, embellishing the individual parts with ferns and flowers and lace. Their faces seemed almost childlike, waving hair decked with daisies and ribbons.

Stefan held the petals of a rose in his palm, the wind

fluttering them gently, stirring their scent, which reminded him of Rose. He had to leave, and Rose's expression the night of their dinner haunted him. She'd hurt him—thinking that her body was only for his play, his enjoyment, and that his heart didn't come with the mix. In French, he'd told her of his love many times during those evening calls; he'd told her of how he felt holding her close, their skin hot with desire, their bodies shaking, and yet his heart had ruled him—for Stefan had found that he was a man who could only make love when he cared deeply.

"The girls should keep Rose long enough for us to get the job done, Stefan. We've got plenty of time. After Mary Lou's baby shower, a bunch of the girls will go down to the Lizard Lounge to top off the night. Rose usually goes with them. So what's to eat, Stefan? Nothing fancy, I hope, maybe just some cold cut sandwiches? These statues are heavy things," Henry said as he put his shoulder against a four-foot faerie holding a wand and muscled it upright.

"Rose will love them," Larry said as he sat down on the ground to study the statues in the rose garden. "Faeries were all she had to comfort her years ago. She gave me a black eye for laughing at her, and she was right to do it. I'm teaching my boys to be more sensitive. Glad you asked us to help, Stefan. Rose deserves nice things."

Stefan prayed he wasn't adding to Rose's fear by placing the statues in her garden, just as he wanted to place his love in her heart. He hadn't meant to sound so cold and hard—*Did you think, my darling, that I would want your body and not your heart?*

He'd sounded as if he were making a business acquisition, but the sting went deep—that Rose would think so little of him. The panic in her wide blue eyes had told him not to push the matter, and he'd hoped that the rose garden faeries would add a gentler persuasion to his case for romance. He'd been very careful not to give Rose gifts because she was still simmering over his refusal to accept payment for roofing her house. He'd torn up the check she'd written for his day of work at the store. He discovered that she was very determined to give an "equalizing" gift when one was given, but the several hundred pound statues weren't easily returned. They were set in concrete, a permanent fixture as was his love. He wanted her to think of him when he was away—and he would have to leave soon.

The men settled down to drink beer and eat bratwursts on buns, slathered with good mustard. Larry and Henry, old friends who had grown up with Rose, cared very deeply for her, and Stefan enjoyed listening to their Rose-stories.

Around midnight, when they were all lying flat on the lawn, studying the moon above, Mrs. Wilkins called, "If you boys don't hurry up and leave, Rose will be home soon and find you snockered in her garden. You're a nice man, Stefan Donatien."

"He sure is," Larry said very slowly and distinctly.

"Sure is," Henry added, seemingly pleased with his loud belch.

"I love Rose, and I love you guys, too," Stefan returned, feeling very mellow as he lay on the ground with his friends. He balanced his bottle of beer on his stomach and studied the faeries surrounding them. They were in different poses, their wings arching, almost fluttering, holding gifts of flowers and birdbaths and sundials, and love. He could almost see them kissing freckles all over Rose's long, delectable body. He wanted her to have something to remember him by when he left on his business trip. "Good job, men," he said.

"She'll love them, but she gets uppity sometimes when

people give her things...because she doesn't want anyone feeling sorry for her,'' Mrs. Wilkins said, coming to settle on the old wooden bench. ''I think you're feeling something other than that and this is a nice way to show her how much you love her. It's unique and sweet, and I'd like to tell you a few stories about Rose, so you'll understand her pride better. She's a giver, you see. She's wound through our lives, a beautiful caring girl, who became even more considerate as a woman. You could always count on Rose in a hard spot, like when I had those bouts of pneumonia. She was right there, taking me to the doctor, taking care of me, like she has other people in Waterville. She spreads kindness like sunshine, and that's why we call her 'The Love Spinner.' But she hasn't learned that in taking gifts, she is also giving.''

She took her scissors and snipped lengths of blue ribbon. ''There, if we tie these around the faeries, they'll seem more like gifts. This blue is the exact shade of Rose's eyes. Got any more bratwursts?''

Stefan served more bratwurst and more beer and settled down into a mellow expectation of how much Rose would like his surprise. With the air sweet around him, and images of Rose steaming nicely to his caresses, Stefan sighed happily. ''I think I love all of you,'' he stated grandly.

''Uh...you're okay, too,'' Larry said after a look at Henry.

''And Rose?'' Mrs. Wilkins prompted.

''Rose is my delight, my dessert, and my life. She glows when she smiles, and opens the sunshine of my heart. She holds it in the palm of her hand and I can only breathe when I am near her. Like good cheese and wine, she will only grow better with time. I am a happy man. I adore her. Every freckle and every scent and every look and—''

Henry frowned at Stefan. ''Say, Steve, could you say

something romantic in French so I could make points with my wife? After watching you with Rose, she thinks I need to study your technique.''

Stefan taught Larry and Henry endearments, and as they curled over his lips and drifted into the night air, he savored the moment when he could whisper them to Rose. He smiled again, and thought of how he would teach Rose and how she would whisper them back to him....

The next morning, Rose stepped out onto her front porch. She did her warm-up stretches for running and sailed out of the front yard. She thought of the tense moments between Yvette and Stefan. Rose decided to call Yvette and Estelle and make certain they knew how much Stefan loved them. He always seemed so strong—Rose wondered if they knew how much he needed them in his life, how he needed to be needed. Rose decided to visit Leroy and explain how important it was for Stefan to help those he loved, and to see that they were treated gently. Rose's needs ran to seeing that Stefan wasn't hurt; she wanted his life to be safe, even though she wouldn't be in it when he returned to the city.

She'd hurt Stefan's feelings that night after they'd made love; she'd seen it in the flash of his eyes, the tilt of his head and the set of his jaw. Two nights ago after their reheated dinner, he'd been very silent as he dressed, gave her a brisk kiss on the cheek and walked out of her home. There had been no evening calls, that beautiful language curling around her, and last night she'd missed him all through the night at the Lizard. She kept wishing for him, wanting him to hold her. It should be so easy to tell him she loved him, but it wasn't. She thought of how she could hurt him when the panic set in—her fear of loving too much.

Stefan surged down the street and soon ran at her side. This morning he wore sunglasses and he hadn't shaved. She remembered the scrape of his beard against her skin, the exotic texture of man. When he didn't speak, Rose asked, "Having a good day?"

"Hmm," he returned darkly, clearly not wanting to indulge in conversation. He glanced down at the blue ribbon trailing out of his pocket and jammed it back in without explanation.

He smiled briefly, as if he were both satisfied and anticipating whatever memories the ribbon stirred. *But he wasn't speaking to her. He was preparing to end their summer. That's all that it was—a summer love…he wasn't a teenager anymore…she could adapt to this…life moved on…* Rose wanted to make ending their affair easy for him, though she would remember him forever. "You'll feel better when you're back at the helm. You know, steady at the rudder, and all that business talk."

The mirrored sunglasses flashed down at her and Stefan's taut mouth did not resemble a happy lover's. Rose decided this wasn't the morning for talk. Then he sailed off and left her with old Walt, who was panting and tired— and Rose ached. "I love him, of course," she whispered to old Walt. "But you see this is for the best, don't you? Stefan deserves someone who isn't going to panic at the thought of commitment. Estelle is in college now and he'll be going back to the city, and I'll be staying here with you, and life will go on the same as always."

Life went on that morning at the paint store, the same as always for Rose Granger. She moved through the sales as if she were a robot, and knew that every day after Stefan left would be the same. He'd become a part of her life— the morning jogging, the late-night calls, those steamy, soul-shattering kisses— Stefan's emotions ran deep, despite his sometimes cool, controlled exterior. She'd hurt him; there had been that tilt of his head, the arrogance and pride in his too soft tone. *Do you think that I would want your body, and not your heart?*

Then at midmorning, Stefan carried a tray into the store and walked back into the storeroom without speaking. She hurried back to see him, to explain how she'd miss him and that things were for the better, and— She looked at the tray filled with crepes and strawberries, coffee and a beautiful rose. ''For me?'' she asked, delighted that he would think of her.

Then her delight shifted into wary expectation—*the beautiful food was Stefan's way of softening the end of their interlude, and that's all it was,* Rose repeated to herself. *An interlude that both knew would end.*

''Danny let me make crepes this morning. They called them 'Steve's pancakes,' but it is no matter. They were a success with the breakfast crowd, and these are for you for helping me resolve those first yelling matches.'' His boyish, triumphant smile dazzled her and while she wasn't thinking of the summer ending, filling herself with how beautiful he looked, Stefan closed the storeroom door and locked it.

''I'm really hungry—'' Rose began. Her body vibrated at his dark, intense look as he moved toward her, tugging her into his arms.

''I am hungry, too. For you,'' he whispered huskily as his hands ran over her, and his mouth came down to meet hers. Because she needed the taste of him, because she loved him and knew that time ran short between them, Rose locked her arms around him, pouring herself into the kiss.

Stefan tensed and slowly eased her away, sweeping the tendrils that had escaped her braids back from her face.

He studied her flushed, upturned face, her closed lids and sensitive, well-kissed lips. ''You want me now?''

He always reacted so well, she thought. His tone held surprise, amusement and hunger and anticipation. Rose licked her lips and looked at his body, wondering where to start— ''Start here,'' Stefan whispered and touched his lips.

Ten

The next time Rose saw Stefan, it was at closing time. She looked out of the store's windows to the sidewalk where he had parked the big leased black Town Car he used for traveling to the airport. He wore those mirrored sunglasses, and the wind tugged at his expensive dress shirt and slacks. He looked nothing like Danny's cook or her lover. Stefan had that lean, stiletto look of a fierce, determined knight going off to battle, already leaning into it, his mind preoccupied with specifics. He glanced impatiently at the expensive watch on his wrist, and Rose's heart began to ache. When he looked up to the dark gray clouds as if he couldn't wait to be off, *she knew that it was closing time between them.*

She forced herself to swallow, her throat gone dry and tight. There would be the usual nicey-nicey talk, the explanations that didn't really need to be made. She'd known all the while that he'd be leaving, once business called him back to Chicago. She fought running and hiding, pain streaking through her. She damned herself for wanting him so, for being so selfish as to take some part of life for herself.

He'd called during the afternoon, but she'd been too busy. He'd been hesitant to tell her what bothered him, and she'd said she'd call him back. Rose inhaled and wished she'd closed the store and taken the time, because now she had to paste a smile on her face when her heart was breaking. She smiled brightly as Stefan entered the door and came toward her. He wouldn't see the tears she guarded closely. She would see him off and step back into the dull reality and safety of her life. "Hi, Stefan. How goes it?" she asked cheerfully.

He'd been so passionate this morning, growling playfully and teasing and hungry for her, just as she wanted him. But the hours had shifted and reality had come to call....

He took off the glasses and his eyes were dark and stormy. She could almost feel his touch, his body as it riveted and completed hers this morning. She could almost hear his chuckle as he held her limp body close and safe on the storeroom's picnic table. *You knew this time would come. Be a good sport, and let him go. Don't get mad. Don't cry. Don't make him feel as if he needs to stay because of you. Stefan is doing the best that he can and you're not going to interfere in his life. What were you thinking?*

"I'll be back," he stated firmly.

"Sure," she returned with a smile that didn't show her breaking heart. She started to study the cardboard advertisement that she'd just unbalanced with her elbow, but her hands shook and it tumbled off the counter.

Stefan picked it up and watched her as he replaced it. He ran his hand through his hair and glanced at his watch and studied her. "I would like you to come with me."

Why prolong the ending? Why not make a clean break? "I've got work to do. You know how it is."

She sounded too chirpy, too happy, and she avoided Stefan's study of her expression as she began clearing the cash machine. "It's business. I've just got time to make my flight," he said quietly. "I wanted to tell you this morning, but I was so—"

Hungry for her. But then she wasn't exactly calm, and had torn his T-shirt to kiss that beautiful chest and place her body against his. The old picnic table in the back would always hold a memory of moving over Stefan—

"Sure. See you." Rose couldn't bear any more. "Look, let's just leave it, okay? No long goodbyes, no promises, no future together. I understood from the start what I was getting into—that you would be leaving and that we had just…intersected at a time when we both needed—"

"I love you, Rose," Stefan said quietly. "I'll be back."

The admission broadsided her, hanging in the air between them. "You don't have to say that. There's no price tag on what we've had. I'm a big girl, Stefan. I know when the ball game is over and there is no need to make it easier for me. Go on, take care of business."

Stefan's jaw tensed. "I'll be back," he repeated darkly. "And we'll settle this between us."

"Sure. For holidays and vacations. That will be nice. It's settled. See you." Then because her heart could not bear more, Rose turned and ran out the back door. She ignored Stefan's call and ran as fast as she could into the woods near town. She scrambled up the old tree where she hid from life long ago and let the tears flow.

After a time, just after sunset, her father came to stand below her. He looked up at her and called softly, "Rose? He's gone. You can come down now. There's something you should see."

Rose hesitated; she knew how she looked—torn by emotions, her face streaked with tears, her hands and knees scraped by the climb. Then because she didn't want to worry him more, she made her way down the tree. "I'm just fine, Dad. Honest."

"Sure," he said in a wry, disbelieving tone. He took her hand as they walked back into Waterville on a course they'd walked many times. "You always are, aren't you, kitten?"

"This is silly of me, getting all worked up like I didn't expect him to leave. Is this how it felt? When Mom left?"

Maury shook his head. "No. Your mother left with another man. Stefan left because he holds other peoples' lives in his hands, in his decisions. Families depend on him, and retirees need him to protect their pensions. He's a powerful businessman, Rose, but he's also just a man. He'll be back. Everything will be fine, you'll see."

They walked to their front gate and Maury said, "Let's go around back. It's pretty out there in the rose garden. Your mother named you 'Rose' because it was the flower she loved best. I think she tried to stay, for your sake."

He watched Rose for a moment as she stared at the faeries in the moonlit garden. They would be there when the fiery leaves began to fall and when snow came and when spring came again to the roses. Then Maury left her alone with Stefan's gift. He paused at the back door and watched Rose wander amid the faeries, looking very much like one of them. "He'll come back, Rose," Maury said quietly to the night, because he believed in Stefan.

Rose skimmed her hands over each unique faerie. They were firmly set in concrete, too big to move, too beautiful to dismiss in the moonlight. She wrapped her arms around the largest one and held it close, just as she wished she could hold Stefan now.

She touched a delicately fashioned wing, smoothing it. *What did Stefan's gift mean? Was it a parting gift? Something he thought might ease the break? Dare she believe?*

Then Rose waited for the faeries to answer her questions, but they only smiled softly. "I've got to be careful that I don't interpret this the wrong way, you know," she told them and settled down to discuss her next move, which of course, was to thank Stefan.

He'd said he loved her.... He'd said he loved her. Stefan wasn't a man to say anything he didn't mean.

Rose went into the house and got the old shoe box that was her mother's. It was battered by a young Rose, furious with life. But now it was time to put away the pain and begin living—to be complete as a woman and leave the rest behind. She'd never wanted to get married, despite her engagements, because part of her still mulled the past and feared how she would be as a wife and mother. The memories had dulled, but they remained inside, simmering, until loving Stefan began to open the unresolved past. She had feared commitment, and the pain of losing. She'd wanted to be so strong and independent within her walls that nothing could ever touch her again.

Then Stefan had come into her life—big and bold and sweet—opening and tearing away the past, bit by bit, filling it with beautiful memories. Rose moved carefully through her thoughts, sorting the important from the clutter. It was time to meet life and what it offered, rather than running from it. *I love you,* he'd said and Stefan wasn't a man to toss words easy and free—he always meant what he said. *I love you.*

Rose scrubbed away her tears and leaned against a faerie. If ever she wanted to believe in fairy tales coming true, it was now. "I love you, too," she whispered to her palm and blew the words away into the wind.

The next morning in Chicago, Stefan sat at the Donatien discussion table, his mind on Rose, on her too-bright expression, and on the way she ran from him. Nothing would have been gained by following her and pressing a point she already doubted. And he'd been hurt, too, that her belief in him ran so thin. In the end, he thought it best to give Rose time—one of the hardest decisions of his life.

A hot debate raged between the Donatien businessmen, some of them elderly and steadfast in his father's strict policies. The younger staff presented a new retirement plan and struggled against the "We've always done it this way." The older members had their points and logic, and the two factions weren't agreeing on anything.

Stefan tapped his pen on the table and tried to follow the debate. He was too tired, and not up to the decisions he must make. He'd tried to call Rose until all hours; she wasn't taking his calls, locking herself away in her safe place, away from his love. She'd been stricken when he told her he loved her, and he'd chosen the wrong moment and issued his emotions too hurriedly. But he'd struggled to give her time to adjust, and then there was no time, an elderly retiree calling him with pension problems that affected several hundred other people.

The issues soared back and forth across the table and

Stefan made notes. He found it best to let the tempers rage, clearing the air and getting to the real heart of the issues, rather than the polite cover-ups. He itemized each issue, dissecting it on his yellow pad. He smiled briefly at the small faerie sketches he'd drawn, and picked his way through the latest storm on the discussion table. "Tim isn't going anywhere. He's made his mistakes and learned from them. He has years of service at Donatien's and I stand behind him," he said quietly. "You're not moving me on this issue."

The older businessmen nodded sagely, because when Stefan's father sounded like that, there was no arguing.

Megan, his secretary, moved close to whisper, "Private call. Line one. It's her. A Miss Rose Granger. Shall I say you'll call her back?"

Stefan knew the value of staying with heated debates and not leaving the room at a crucial time—but he wanted to talk with Rose. "I'll take the call here."

"Here?" Megan's tone reflected her astonishment— Donatien business meetings were never to be interrupted with personal calls—Miss Rose Granger must have indicated she had personal business with Stefan.

"Stefan here," he said and waited for Rose to speak. Had she seen the faeries? What would she think? Would she believe his love? Had he terrified her, telling her of his love, giving her gifts of his heart?

"I can't pay for all these," she said finally. She spoke as if she didn't know where to start and that was the top issue on her mind. "Larry and Henry said they were custom made."

"They're a gift from me. To keep you company while I'm away." Her silence said she was weighing his words and that struck Stefan's pride. There was always that doubt in her, that tiny nagging lack of trust.

"I have nothing to give you," Rose said quietly.

"But of course you do, my darling. And this isn't a gift to be equaled, Rose. It's one of the heart and freely given." Stefan ignored the silence around his board table, the downcast faces, the tense poses that said they were listening closely. Stefan studied them, the staunch, elderly peers of his father who wanted to change nothing, and resisted women into the mix. The women at the table had earned their place and the younger men were all part of a family—his family. Estelle had expressed interest in entering the business, in managing it. It would take her years to win over the old guard, but then Estelle had learned a few things from Rose. Simple things, like listening and that gentle persuasion.

He saw no reason not to throw his "Rose" problems on the table with the rest of the current business. "I love this woman. I want to marry her," Stefan told them, making certain that Rose could hear, because he'd punched the loudspeaker button. "I gave her faerie statues for her rose garden and now she wants to know how much to pay me. What do you think of that?"

Stunned silence flattened the room. Stefan Donatien was his father's son, bred to business, not to emotions or romantic gifts. His heritage was grim and weighty. He smiled at Rose's slight gasp at the other end of the line. "I love you, Rose. Get used to it. I'm not going to be an ex-fiancé. I want to be your husband, if you'll have me. I asked your father some time ago, because after all, I am a traditional man. I have his permission to ask you. All we have to do—you and I—is to settle the fine points between—like if you love me and want to marry me. We'll live in Waterville, of course. We'll take whatever time you need.''

He smiled grimly at Rose's next gasp. "Is everyone listening to this?" she asked unevenly.

"I have nothing to hide. You make me very happy." He hadn't meant to hurl his intentions at her that way, but he was still new at separating business and love. "You're very good at relationships, the best at facilitating tense situations. I'm in a discussion now where no one wants to budge. Please help me, Rose."

He smiled and waited, because Rose always knew the right answers when it came to people. She was wandering through his "I love you," and her fears, but she never let anyone down who needed her. He held up his hand when the staunch old guard looked like they might object.

"Well," Rose said softly, thoughtfully. "First of all— I think you should send out for ice-cream cones. They always make things better. And if the weather is beautiful there, as it is here—a bright fall day—open the window to let the wind blow in and clear away the tension. And listen to the life passing through on the sidewalk below. I think by the time you've done all that, and talked about the different flavors of ice cream, everyone might be flowing along in the same track."

"That's a good idea. Thank you, Rose. I miss you." Stefan nodded to his secretary, who blinked and silently mouthed, "Ice-cream cones?" He nodded again and she hurriedly left the room.

"Do you need me for anything else, Stefan?" Rose asked over the loudspeaker in a professional tone.

"Yes," he said huskily and smiled again at the pause.

"Oh. Bye," she returned in that breathless tone he loved. He inhaled briefly when the line clicked off. Then

Stefan started to work, settling the issues, because he wanted to go home to Rose.

When his secretary came into the room again, her expression concerned, Stefan nodded. He picked up the telephone and smiled as he heard Rose's voice. "I'm not happy," she said. "I don't know how to handle all this."

"It won't do for our children to have an unhappy mother," Stefan said, enjoying the play. He listened to Rose's uneven breathing and imagined her steamy, quivery look like just before she tore his T-shirt to have him. "I'll be home soon and we'll fix that."

"Oh. Goodbye," she said airily after a slight hesitation, and the line clicked off.

Stefan looked around the table, at the older, rigid faces, silently admonishing him for his lack of business protocol. The younger ones were softer and Stefan relaxed a bit as the women smiled fondly at him—they'd always been a little uncertain of him and now that gap seemed to be closing. "We'll manage, and we'll succeed," he said firmly. "I forbid anything else."

How could Stefan be so confident of her? Of them? Rose wondered as she spent hours amid the faeries he had given her, each one perfect—except the one with the tutu and that was slanted oddly, her gauzy panties showing. Each day Rose wondered what she could give Stefan, and the leaves of the oaks shading the faeries gave no answers.

The casseroles didn't come to her as they usually did after a breakup. Life was odd and lonely, and she waited for Yvette's tidbits of Stefan. He sent her a tiny, perfect pin, one with diamonds on the fragile faerie wing. It was elegant and contrasted her T-shirt, but she wore it anyway—at night in her rose garden with the faeries. She sent him a thank-you note, because that seemed very proper to do. *What could she give Stefan? Was it possible he really loved her and that he was coming back?*

Another week took Rose into mid-September and Stefan wasn't calling. She knew he was very busy and giving her time to think. Yet all she could think of was needing him close and safe. To show her father that Maggie White was perfectly welcome in their family, Rose threw a swing dance party at the Granger home. Yvette and Leroy attended and moved together as if they had all their lives. Leroy obviously adored Yvette. Maggie had centered on Maury and wasn't looking at other men—a soft, well-loved look replaced her chic, manhunting one.

While the music played loudly and Mrs. Wilkins took care of the refreshment table, it seemed to be a perfect time for Rose to call Stefan—just to hear that deep drawl, his beautiful accent. Instead when he answered, his tone was weary. She wanted to make him feel better and also to relieve the nagging need to— "Oh, hi. Just thought I'd call to tell you that I love you, too.... And your gifts are far too expensive, but I love them anyway. Bye."

There was silence and then the rush of French seemed to be in the swearing mode. "You are there, and I am here, and you would pick such a time to tell me?" he demanded unevenly.

"Tit for tat, equality and all that," she said, defending her right to equal what he had said.

Stefan's voice was uneven and threaded heavily with his accent. "I wanted to propose to you differently—I wanted to see you alone, but in Waterville there seems to be very little 'alone.'"

"It just came to me slowly, no big flashes of thunder

or anything. But it's there, in my heart, and it's good and strong.''

Rose listened to the laughter and music coming from the living room. It all seemed very right that she should call Stefan at a time like this—when all the people she loved were enjoying themselves. ''Am I on the loudspeaker? I hear other men there. You're probably in a business meeting. It's too late for that, Stefan. You need your rest because when you come home—''

''We speak privately,'' Stefan stated huskily. ''Proceed with your definition of the activity.''

''Well, then, I should tell you how much I love you. Maybe a part of me was always waiting for you, my prince. I moved into the bigger bedroom, because I want to remember you with me. How much I want to touch you and feel you close and naked beside me. I want to kiss you—on the lips—have patience with me, because I'm new to this. I want to nibble a bit on your lips and then on your throat and then on your ears—and blow a bit there—''

Rose blew softly into the telephone for effect and she smiled at the slight hissing of Stefan's breath as though he were stunned and inhaling sharply. She liked shocking Stefan; he reacted so beautifully. She was woman, feminine, strong and erotic, and leaned back against the kitchen wall to concentrate on her best effort. Rose smiled as she continued to explain how she wanted to love Stefan. ''That's enough,'' he said roughly after a time and she knew that nothing was more enjoyable than teasing him.

In the background, a man asked, ''Stefan, are you feeling all right? You look like you might have a fever.''

''Good night, *ma chérie,*'' Stefan said softly. ''I will think of you in your new environment. I will try to accommodate your specifications to my utmost ability at our next meeting.''

She turned with a smile to replace the telephone and found Mrs. Wilkins fanning herself as she stared at Rose. ''Goodness, Rose. I'll bet you never talked to the other boys like that.''

Rose grinned, her all-woman feeling at sky-high level. Mrs. Wilkins had been a part of her life forever—she was a dear heart whom Rose trusted. ''Nope, never have. I think I might be pretty good at it, too. Stefan had this funny little strangled sound that I've never heard before. Oh, he's so much fun!''

''That's what I've been waiting to hear. You never were really excited about those other boys. You never blossomed and floated on air like you do now. You'll be married and pregnant before you know it…. And now I think I'll put a little gin in the punch, drink it and let myself have an old-fashioned good cry…a happy one.''

''It just came to me so gently, loving Stefan, that I hadn't realized how much I do love him. I love him so much that I fear nothing, that I know he and I will survive—together. I know the weight of responsibility and Stefan carries such a heavy burden, not exactly of his making. He needs me in a soft way, the way a man needs a woman. I've waited all this time for him, just him. He's very emotional, you know, and he worries too much. Stefan is a dynamic man and I know that waiting for me couldn't have been easy. I intend to make that up to him.''

Mrs. Wilkins blinked away the tears in her eyes. ''He's getting a very special person, and he knows it. Um, dear? Does he know you can't cook?''

Waterville had waited for the wedding of Rose Granger, and everyone came to the October event. In her faerie garden, Stefan and Rose took their vows beneath their fiery oaks. Stefan was very formal, firmly hiding his excitement, and Rose's flowing, soft gown was designed by Yvette and Estelle.

Stefan's whiskey-brown eyes were too bright, but his hands were firm on hers as he slid his wedding band onto her finger. When her ring was upon his finger, he stared at it as if he couldn't believe she had placed it there. He spoke unevenly, huskily telling her of his love, and she pledged hers to him without hesitation.

Their kiss was soft and told of the years to come, of the life they would build together.

Then Walt loped into the garden and sat between them, looking up expectantly as they were pronounced man and wife. Because Walt knew he had a home with Rose—he always had.

Black limousines lined the side street, because the front street and yard around Rose's house was filled with smiling, happy people. They surged toward the bride and groom and the tables piled high with Stefan's and Danny's food. Danny's wedding cake towered above the platters of French cuisine and fried green tomatoes and hamburgers and French fries. After snapshots, Stefan, Yvette and Estelle moved into action. Stefan rolled up his sleeves and began serving in his elaborate, flourished waiter-way, and Rose sat beside Walt, listened to congratulations, and wondered about her wedding night. ''The missing ingredient in all this, Walt old buddy, is that Stefan hasn't made love to me for a very, very long time.''

Then Stefan paused in serving his petit fours and met her eyes across the garden. The riveting shock was enough to assure her that he wanted her desperately. She decided that was the time to tug up her beautiful feminine gown and slowly, enticingly remove her lace garter.

While staring hungrily at his new bride, Stefan hadn't realized that the tray had tipped and the desserts were plopping to the ground. Sensing food, Walt hurried to make the best of the day. "We're leaving," Stefan announced curtly, and made his way to her. From the narrowed, hot way he was looking at her, Rose knew there wasn't much time. She threw her bouquet to Maggie, who blushed prettily and leaned against Maury, who tightened his arm around her. As if giving his blessing, Stefan tossed Rose's garter to Leroy, who promptly tugged it onto his upper arm and grinned at her before he stole a kiss from Yvette.

Stefan picked up Rose and strode to his pickup with her. When Rose opened the door, Walt hopped in. He sat between them as they drove off, tin cans rattling as the crowd was silent. Some were thinking that she wouldn't have time for them anymore, not with a new husband and that big new addition he'd just built on to the Smith's farmhouse. Then, from the hot-eyed look of the hungry groom, she'd probably have that flock of children she deserved and even less time.

She'd wound through their lives like the multicolored ribbons tied to the faeries and fluttering in the slight breeze. Rose deserved the best possible, and from the look of her groom, she wouldn't be lacking for love.

On the other hand, Rose wasn't going anywhere, except for business trips Stefan had to make to the city. Eventually his daughter would take over some of his burden, and Waterville would still have Rose. And best of all, she would be happy and they'd get to see her life become even richer. Then Henry let out a cheer, holding his glass of champagne high. "Here's to Rose and her faeries and her prince."

"This is quite elaborate, isn't it?" Rose asked as Stefan closed the wooden barn doors behind them. The huge old barn had sat empty, gray and weathered for years on the far side of the Smith farm. Now it had been cleaned, and in the exact airy center was a very spiffy new camper. Walt trotted around the barn, examining the different smells, while Stefan picked Rose up in his arms and walked determinedly toward the deluxe camper.

"This should take care of the lack of privacy here. I want no interruptions," he said grimly as Rose opened the camper door and he carried her inside. A moment later, he opened the door and with a flourish, placed a rug on the barn floor with dog food and water. "No," he said firmly to Walt, who was hoping for an invitation inside.

Stefan turned and closed the camper door, locking it. The soft light seemed to embrace his bride as she stood still, staring at him. "I love you, Stefan. I didn't think this would ever happen for me, and now it has."

She looked stunned, a reflection of his own emotions, which mixed with his hunger for her now. "Don't be afraid, Rose," he said. "I love you. We're going to have a wonderful life together, and I'll never leave you."

"I know. You love me, and I love you, and dreams come true. It's all pretty amazing how the pieces fit together. Now how do I get out of this dress?" she asked softly.

"I believe I can help you with that, Mrs. Donatien," Stefan offered and moved toward her.

Later, when she was soft and draped over him, her toes playing with his, Rose smoothed his chest and nestled close. "You can tell me now, the gift that you said I gave to you?—other than the obvious."

Stefan was silent so long that Rose thought he might be resting from the event they had just shared. He stroked her hair and spoke softly. "You made me see that my father's dreams and fears aren't mine. That life waits outside business and work, that each breath is rich and full, when you want it to be…. You give me peace and happiness and the joy in living. You make me look forward to each day, and anchor my heart and my soul. You fill me with one look, soothe me with one touch, and you make me feel like I am a better person than I am. You give me courage and strength and wisdom."

"Goodness. How do I do all that?"

"By being just you, Rose."

Stefan looked into Rose's eyes and knew that life with her would be full and rich, buttery and smooth, with a delicate, loving texture that would always be fresh, the spices perfect and exciting.

* * * * *

Don't miss
TALLCHIEF: THE HUNTER,
the next compelling romance
in Cait London's popular miniseries
THE TALLCHIEFS
available in February 2002.

Feel like a star with Silhouette.

We will fly you and a guest to New York City for an exciting weekend stay at a glamorous 5-star hotel. Experience a refreshing day at one of New York's trendiest spas and have your photo taken by a professional. Plus, receive $1,000 U.S. spending money!

Flowers...long walks...dinner for two... how does Silhouette Books make romance come alive for you?

Send us a script, with 500 words or less, along with visuals (only drawings, magazine cutouts or photographs or combination thereof). Show us how Silhouette Makes Your Love Come Alive. Be creative and have fun. No purchase necessary. All entries must be clearly marked with your name, address and telephone number. All entries will become property of Silhouette and are not returnable. **Contest closes September 28, 2001.**

Please send your entry to: **Silhouette Makes You a Star!**

In U.S.A.	In Canada
P.O. Box 9069	P.O. Box 637
Buffalo, NY, 14269-9069	Fort Erie, ON, L2A 5X3

Look for contest details on the next page, by visiting www.eHarlequin.com or request a copy by sending a self-addressed envelope to the applicable address above. Contest open to Canadian and U.S. residents who are 18 or over. Void where prohibited.

Silhouette®
Where love comes alive™

Our lucky winner's photo will appear in a Silhouette ad. Join the fun!

SRMYAS1

HARLEQUIN "SILHOUETTE MAKES YOU A STAR!" CONTEST 1308
OFFICIAL RULES
NO PURCHASE NECESSARY TO ENTER

1. To enter, follow directions published in the offer to which you are responding. Contest begins June 1, 2001, and ends on September 28, 2001. Entries must be postmarked by September 28, 2001, and received by October 5, 2001. Enter by hand-printing (or typing) on an 8 ½" x 11" piece of paper your name, address (including zip code), contest number/name and attaching a script containing <u>500 words</u> or less, <u>along with drawings, photographs or magazine cutouts, or combinations thereof</u> (i.e., collage) <u>on no larger than 9" x 12"</u> piece of paper, describing how the <u>Silhouette books make romance come alive for you.</u> Mail via first-class mail to: Harlequin "Silhouette Makes You a Star!" Contest 1308, (in the U.S.) P.O. Box 9069, Buffalo, NY 14269-9069, (in Canada) P.O. Box 637, Fort Erie, Ontario, Canada L2A 5X3. Limit one entry per person, household or organization.

2. Contests will be judged by a panel of members of the Harlequin editorial, marketing and public relations staff. Fifty percent of criteria will be judged against script and fifty percent will be judged against drawing, photographs and/or magazine cutouts. Judging criteria will be based on the following:

   - Sincerity—25%
   - Originality and Creativity—50%
   - Emotionally Compelling—25%

   In the event of a tie, duplicate prizes will be awarded. Decisions of the judges are final.

3. All entries become the property of Torstar Corp. and may be used for future promotional purposes. Entries will not be returned. No responsibility is assumed for lost, late, illegible, incomplete, inaccurate, nondelivered or misdirected mail.

4. Contest open only to residents of the U.S. <u>(except Puerto Rico)</u> and Canada who are 18 years of age or older, and is void wherever prohibited by law; all applicable laws and regulations apply. Any litigation within the Province of Quebec respecting the conduct or organization of a publicity contest may be submitted to the Régie des alcools, des courses et des jeux for a ruling. Any litigation respecting the awarding of a prize may be submitted to the Régie des alcools, des courses et des jeux only for the purpose of helping the parties reach a settlement. Employees and immediate family members of Torstar Corp. and D. L. Blair, Inc., their affiliates, subsidiaries and all other agencies, entities and persons connected with the use, marketing or conduct of this contest are not eligible to enter. Taxes on prizes are the sole responsibility of the winner. Acceptance of any prize offered constitutes permission to use winner's name, photograph or other likeness for the purposes of advertising, trade and promotion on behalf of Torstar Corp., its affiliates and subsidiaries without further compensation to the winner, unless prohibited by law.

5. Winner will be determined no later than November 30, 2001, and will be notified by mail. Winner will be required to sign and return an Affidavit of Eligibility/Release of Liability/Publicity Release form within 15 days after winner notification. Noncompliance within that time period may result in disqualification and an alternative winner may be selected. All travelers must execute a Release of Liability prior to ticketing and must possess required travel documents (e.g., passport, photo ID) where applicable. Trip must be booked by December 31, 2001, and completed within one year of notification. No substitution of prize permitted by winner. Torstar Corp. and D. L. Blair, Inc., their parents, affiliates and subsidiaries are not responsible for errors in printing of contest, entries and/or game pieces. In the event of printing or other errors that may result in unintended prize values or duplication of prizes, all affected game pieces or entries shall be null and void. **Purchase or acceptance of a product offer does not improve your chances of winning.**

6. Prizes: (1) Grand Prize—A 2-night/3-day trip for two (2) to New York City, including round-trip coach air transportation nearest winner's home and hotel accommodations (double occupancy) at The Plaza Hotel, a glamorous afternoon makeover at <u>a trendy New York spa</u>, $1,000 in U.S. spending money and an opportunity to <u>have a professional photo taken and appear in a Silhouette advertisement</u> (approximate retail value: $7,000). (10) Ten Runner-Up Prizes of gift packages (retail value $50 ea.). Prizes consist of only those items listed as part of the prize. Limit one prize per person. Prize is valued in U.S. currency.

7. For the name of the winner (available after December 31, 2001) send a self-addressed, stamped envelope to: Harlequin "Silhouette Makes You a Star!" Contest 1197 Winners, P.O. Box 4200 Blair, NE 68009-4200 or you may access the www.eHarlequin.com Web site through February 28, 2002.

Contest sponsored by Torstar Corp., P.O Box 9042, Buffalo, NY 14269-9042.

SRMYAS2

COMING NEXT MONTH

#1387 THE MILLIONAIRE COMES HOME—Mary Lynn Baxter
Man of the Month
Millionaire Denton Hardesty returned to his hometown only to find himself
face-to-face with Grace Simmons—the lover he'd never forgotten. Spending
time at Grace's bed-and-breakfast, Denton realized he wanted to rekindle the
romance he'd broken off years ago. Now all he had to do was convince Grace
that *this* time he intended to stay...forever.

#1388 COMANCHE VOW—Sheri WhiteFeather
In keeping with the old Comanche ways, Nick Bluestone promised to marry
his brother's widow, Elaina Myers-Bluestone, and help raise her daughter.
Love wasn't supposed to be part of the bargain, but Nick couldn't deny the
passion he found in Elaina's embrace. Could Nick risk his heart and claim
Elaina as his wife...*in every way?*

#1389 WHEN JAYNE MET ERIK—Elizabeth Bevarly
20 Amber Court
That's me, bride-on-demand Jayne Pembroke, about to get hitched to the
one and only drop-dead gorgeous Erik Randolph. The proposal was simple
enough—one year together and we'd both get what we wanted. But one taste
of those spine-tingling kisses and I was willing to bet things were going to get a
whole lot more complicated!

#1390 FORTUNE'S SECRET DAUGHTER—Barbara McCauley
Fortunes of Texas: The Lost Heirs
When store owner Holly Douglas rescued injured bush pilot Guy Blackwolf
after his plane crashed into a lake by her home, she found herself irresistibly
attracted to the charming rogue and his magnetic kisses. But would she be able
to entrust her heart to Guy once she learned the secret he had kept from her?

#1391 SLEEPING WITH THE SULTAN—Alexandra Sellers
Sons of the Desert: The Sultans
When powerful and attractive Sheikh Ashraf abducted actress Dana Morningstar
aboard his luxury yacht, he claimed that he was desperately in love with her and
wanted the chance to gain her love in return. Dana knew she shouldn't trust
Ashraf—but could she resist his passionate kisses and tender seduction?

#1392 THE BRIDAL ARRANGEMENT—Cindy Gerard
Lee Savage had promised to marry and take care of Ellie Shiloh in accordance
with her father's wishes. Lee soon became determined to show his innocent
young bride the world she had always been protected from. But he hadn't
counted on Ellie's strength and courage to show him a thing or two...about
matters of the heart.

SDCNM0801